# The Darkest Hour

ALASKAN HEARTS
BOOK SEVEN

MELISSA STORM

**Editor**: Megan Harris
**Cover**: Daqri Bernardo, Covers by Combs
**Proofreader**: Jasmine Jordan

*To Angi*
*Who loved this story first.*

# About this Book

Sofia Stepanov believes in right and wrong, but she doesn't necessarily believe in following the rules. When she finds a wolf hybrid being illegally kept and abused by its captors, she vows to come back and free him herself.

Soon the exhilaration of one successful mission leads to many more, leading Sofia to set her sights on the most ambitious rescue yet. It also leads her straight into the path of a handsome police officer who has been tasked with bringing Anchorage's serial dognapper to justice.

Will Sofia complete her vigilante rescue without a hitch, or will Hunter catch her before she can?

# One

Sofia Stepanov's journey toward happily ever after started the way so many do—with a beautiful, tortured pair of eyes staring straight into her soul.

She gulped before taking a closer look. These eyes didn't belong to a charming prince, but rather a mottled gray dog chained to a stake in somebody's front yard.

*Help me,* those striking amber orbs begged, but Sofia rolled past the stop sign and continued toward her destination. It's not that she was heartless, though sometimes her friends teased that stodgy Sofia kept her heart locked up tight in a tiny box hidden deep within her chest.

She wanted to help the poor, neglected mutt, but what could she do? She was already late for work. She didn't have a lick of experience owning a pet, and stealing was just a touch against the law.

Regardless, Sofia thought about that poor, scraggly creature the whole day, ultimately making a deal with herself. *If I drive past there tonight and he's still out there, then I'll break him free.*

And, sure enough, the dog she'd taken to calling "Wolfie" in her mind remained chained in place when she drove back through the dilapidated Mountain View neighborhood more than eight hours later.

She'd "borrowed" a leash from the mall's pet store on her way home from work, reasoning that she didn't have to pay if it was only meant to be a loan. Besides, she was doing the Lord's work, protecting his creatures and all that.

Yeah, it definitely would have been far worse to do nothing. The universe *wanted* her to free this poor sap of a dog, and so she would.

She drove by the yard a few times just to make sure that no one was home, then parked down the block and began her rescue mission.

Wolfie let out a low whine as she approached. He kept his head and body on the ground, but slowly, hopefully, began to thump his tail in the dirt beneath him.

No bared teeth—a good sign if ever there was one.

Sofia had never kept a pet growing up, then hadn't wanted the added responsibility once she'd finally struck out on her own. Even so, she'd always had a way with animals, especially the downtrodden ones. They seemed to somehow sense a kindred spirit in her which, she had to admit, *was* accurate.

Nobody had ever chained Sofia to a stake, but they'd done plenty of awful things to her growing up. Gossip, rumors, pranks, all the usual mean girl fodder had all been directed squarely at Sofia.

In seventh grade, she'd gone through an adolescent revolution and finally found out exactly who she was meant to be, which unfortunately also meant finding herself as the official Bartlett High outcast. Previously a blonde, pink-cheeked clone of her mother, Sofia had dyed her hair black and never looked back. She'd begun avoiding the sun as if she really were a vampire, like one of the less imaginative rumors about her had claimed.

And now here she was, creeping around at night, getting ready to steal somebody's dog.

Not steal—*rescue*.

She had to remind herself of that over and over again until she was sure she believed it. Sofia was the good guy here. Had always been.

Reaching into her bag, she wrapped her fingers around the food court hotdog she'd picked up for just this purpose.

Wolfie's whining intensified when he saw the snack.

"You want this, boy? Yeah?" Sofia tiptoed up to the dog and handed him the hotdog while she switched the chain for the leash.

*Quick, quick. There. Atta boy.*

Checking that the clasp was secure, she removed a second hotdog from her bag and flashed it before the dog. "We have to hurry, okay? Just follow me, and I'll give you another one of these. Got it?"

Wolfie barked, his tail swinging at a frenzied pace.

"Shhhh," Sofia warned, slowly letting herself back out through the gate with Wolfie in tow. "Let's go."

If anyone saw the dognapping in action, they did nothing to stop it. It was almost too easy. Sofia kept waiting for an angry, gun-waving homeowner or the whir of sirens, but nothing happened. It felt like mere seconds. One moment, she was just passing by, and the next she'd somehow become a dog owner.

Did easy mean right? Well, she guessed time would tell on that one.

So now what?

## Two

Once safely back at home, Sofia coaxed Wolfie into her apartment and offered him a bowl of water. It had been a warm day, making Sofia squirm in her black A-line dress. Wolfie must have been downright miserable out in the sun all day with not a drop of water in sight.

Sure enough, he drank the water in less time than it took Sofia to fill the dish. After refilling it a few times, she grabbed her largest pot from the cabinet under the sink and filled that to the brim with water as well.

Wolfie didn't want to stop. He drank and drank, making Sofia wonder where all that fluid went in such a scrawny dog.

In answer to this question, Wolfie wheezed, coughed, then vomited a clear puddle at her feet.

Apparently that made him feel better, because he began to run around the apartment in fast, tight loops—jumping onto the couch and off, onto the table and off, moving so fast he was little more than a gray blur.

Sofia's head spun. "Wolfie, calm down!" she cried, and surprisingly, he did listen.

Almost at once, the dog dived beneath the table and cowered in fear.

"Oh, I'm sorry. I didn't mean to scare you," she mumbled, crouching down and offering the dog her hand.

Wolfie began to shake violently but didn't resist when Sofia gently lifted her hand to scratch between his ears.

"They really treated you badly, didn't they?" she asked, motioning for the dog to come out from his makeshift cave. "It's okay. I've got you now. C'mon, it's okay."

Slowly, Wolfie came toward her, his posture still stooped, a line of urine trailing behind him.

One thing was for certain: she had been sent to save this dog and she would not be turning him into the shelter where they'd just stick him back in a cage and he'd be passed over for cuter and less frightened puppies.

"There, there. It's okay," she whispered as she ran her fingers through Wolfie's thick coat. Little tufts of fur came out in her hand, but Wolfie seemed to like the physical touch, so she kept talking to him, stroking him, promising him she would take care of him from here on out.

When he started to relax, she grabbed the scissors out of her junk drawer and worked on the mats clinging to his belly and legs. Wolfie shifted and whined, but ultimately let her help him. Already they'd reached some understanding. Already they were becoming a team.

"We need to get you to a vet," she said, studying the angry red mark on the dog's back knee. Was this a sign of abuse? And if it was, would she call in an anonymous tip about Wolfie's former owner?

She didn't want to do anything to risk losing the dog she'd promised to care for, but at the same time, people like this deserved to be punished to the fullest extent of the law. And then some.

After a few brief moments spent weighing her options, Sofia placed a call to her former employee, Liz Benjamin—who now went by Elizabeth Jane.

*Long story.*

"Hey, girl. What's up?" her friend asked, the sound of wind whipping past the speaker.

"Hate to bother you like this, it's just…" Sofia had to choose her words carefully, because whatever story she told Liz now was the one she'd be stuck with going forward. "It's just, I found this dog on my way home from work, and I think he needs to see a vet."

Liz sounded distracted, but not surprised. "You found a dog?"

She gulped before speaking the first of what would surely be many lies about how Wolfie came to be hers. "Yes, he was walking by the side of the highway. I didn't want him to get hit, so I let him into my car. And now I'm kind of fond of the old guy."

"Yeah, I know how that goes," Elizabeth Jane said with a laugh, then after a slight pause, "Umm, most vets are closed by now, but there's an emergency animal hospital in Midtown if you want to swing by there."

"Great, thanks." Sofia could tell her friend's hurried responses that she needed to go. Sofia needed to go herself if she was going to get Wolfie into the vet sometime that night. For all she knew he had ring worm, or rabies, or something even worse. She glanced at the dog, who tilted his head in response.

"Do you want me to come with you?" Liz asked after a brief shuffling on the other end of the line.

Sofia smiled at Wolfie and ran her fingers through his fur once more. "No, I'm sure you have lots to do. I've got this."

Elizabeth Jane sounded relieved. "Well, call me if you need anything. Maybe stop by the ranch with him over the weekend, and I can give you some of Samson's old stuff to get you started as an official dog owner."

"Awesome. Gotta go." Sofia hung up, then pushed herself back to her feet.

Wolfie let her clip him back onto the leash without the bribe of a hotdog, and they were off.

*What had Liz been doing that she needed to keep a secret?* Sofia wondered briefly before opening the window and letting the cooling wind rush through the car.

# Three

S ofia and Wolfie arrived at the Benson Animal Hospital less than half an hour later. The large waiting room sat mostly empty, except for an elderly woman holding a cat carrier in her lap and a man about Sofia's age sitting beside his dog on the other side of the room.

Spotting the other dog, Wolfie let out an excited whine and began to strain against the leash, dragging Sofia with him to the far end of the waiting room.

"Is it okay if we say hello?" she asked the man, hoping that Wolfie wouldn't attack the other dog he so desperately wanted to meet.

"Of course. This is Scout. I'm Hunter. Hunter Burke." The man stood and gestured to the German Shepherd at his side.

Sofia had heard that having a dog helped you meet people, but she was surprised by how soon Wolfie was making new friends for the both of them—especially when those friends were as handsome as the man standing before her. "I'm Sofia, and this is Wolfie," she said with what she hoped was a confident smile.

The dogs sniffed each other, both with tails wagging.

Hunter held out his hand to Sofia, a crooked grin hidden beneath his beard. Sofia had always been a sucker for a man with a bit of scruff. If he had tattoos, too, she'd be a goner.

"New dog owner?" he asked with a knowing tilt of his head. His sandy hair fell onto his forehead, and he reached up to push it back.

Sofia watched the muscles in his arms tighten, then relax again. She even spied a patch of dark ink peeking out from beneath his shirt sleeve. That made it official: Hunter Burke was the perfect specimen of masculinity.

"Is it that obvious?" She suddenly felt very awkward beneath his studious gaze. Had he seen how the dress Sofia had designed hugged all her curves in just the right places? Could he tell that the candy apple red lipstick she wore was the exactly perfect shade to go with her complexion? "About being new to dogs, I mean?"

"Yes, but it's okay. I'm sure you have your hands full with a wolf hybrid. And is he a rescue, too?"

"Wait, wolf hybrid? What makes you say that?"

"His eyes, for one. Also his size. That isn't your standard sled dog. Didn't the rescue organization tell you that?"

"Umm, not really. They mostly just seemed happy to have a home for him." Sofia back-pedaled quickly. She'd already mixed up her story, and she'd hardly had Wolfie for an hour now. This did not bode well for her ability to keep his theft a secret.

"Don't worry. He's probably not a hybrid. That being illegal and all. Besides. I'd hate to have to put a pretty girl like you in jail," Hunter said with a gentle smile that made Sofia's breath hitch.

Had he really just called her pretty? Usually the feminist in her hated being called out on her looks, but from Hunter... *Oh, mama.*

She chanced a smile back at him. Normally, she wasn't so shy around... well, anyone. But something about Hunter and the situation left her a bit speechless.

"Don't worry. I'm only kidding." Hunter reached into his back pocket and pulled out a badge with a laugh. "I always forget that people don't like it when guys like me make jokes like that."

*A cop?* Sofia swallowed the lump forming in her throat. Well, that wasn't good. "Oh," she said.

"Why the frown?" he asked with a chuckle. "I promise I only arrest people who deserve it."

"Yeah." She forced a laugh. Had God set Hunter Burke in her path to remind her that she had obtained Wolfie by illegal means? Was this a test? Should she come clean?

She looked to Wolfie, who was enthusiastically sniffing Scout's butt. No, she couldn't betray her new dog so soon—or ever. She'd made a promise to protect him and couldn't let a guilty conscience get in her way. So, she'd stolen a dog. It wasn't technically legal, but it was the right thing to do. She could have very well saved his life.

Yeah, taking Wolfie had been right. Keeping him was the right call, too.

Hunter spoke up again. "Okay, you seem a bit intimidated. Don't be."

She shifted her eyes from the dogs back to the handsome man standing beside here.

"We're all fighting something, right? Like you. What do you do?" he asked.

"I work at the mall. Clothing store, but I also

design and sell my own fashions on Etsy." Why was she telling him this? She didn't need to justify herself or her job. She just needed to get Wolfie checked out by the vet and then to get them both back home.

"So, you're fighting against bad fashion decisions and nakedness." His eyes flashed with mischief, as if it was his goal to make her squirm.

And squirm she did.

"I... Um..." She felt heat rush to her cheeks and tried to hide her embarrassment.

"Too forward?" He laughed and shook his head. "Yeah, probably. But look, the vet could call either of us back any minute and, well, I don't want to go without at least getting your number or giving you mine."

"Umm, okay." She handed him her phone, wishing he'd been anything other than a cop. Otherwise, she'd be jumping for joy at Hunter's flirtations. "I'll take yours," she said, knowing that she would never, ever call him.

Just then, the back door opened and a woman wearing a white lab coat smiled over at them. "Scout?"

"Well, that's us." Hunter hesitated before placing Sofia's phone back into her hand. They stood so close, she could easily lean forward to kiss him—or he her. But Hunter Burke was not meant for her.

"Bye, Sofia," he said, holding her gaze before finally turning toward the dogs. "Bye, Wolfie. It was nice meeting you both."

Sofia watched in silence as man and his dog disappeared through the door.

*Thank goodness.*

# Four

L uckily, the welt on Wolfie's knee turned out to be a heat spot, but the sore did require a pricey medication in order to clear it up. The vet also gave Sofia a huge list of items she needed to buy for her new life as a dog owner. The thing was so long, it had been printed on both the front and back side of the paper.

*No way I'll be able to afford all this.*

She'd already spent her extra money for the month on a new dressmaker's dummy and a few bolts of fabric that she planned to use for her summer looks.

Sofia knew she should charge more for her designs on Etsy, but she'd always said money wasn't important, that what really mattered was getting people into clothes *she'd* designed. Of course, now as she stared down at this unexpected shopping list, combined with the bill for Wolfie's exam, shots, and after-hours visit, she wished she'd taken a different stance when it came to pricing her online boutique.

But more than that, Sofia wanted to cry.

She'd never been a crier, but at the moment, it seemed as if she'd have to choose between her promise to Wolfie or her budding business as a fashion designer. Both were important to her, and she couldn't picture her life without either. Wolfie needed her just as she needed fashion. Creating the perfect outfit had always been a refuge, a way of celebrating her body instead of feeling confined by it.

A life without her design work would mean being trapped in her dead-end job for eternity—and that would obviously murder her soul.

On the other hand, Wolfie was an actual living thing. He'd been put in her path for a reason. She'd liberated him and thus was now responsible for whatever became of him next. How could she choose something as insignificant as clothing over a living, breathing creature?

There was no way around it. *This sucked.*

Unless...

She'd already "borrowed" a leash from the pet

store. Would it really be so wrong if she took a few other supplies, too? She would pay, once she could afford to, but her next paycheck was practically a full two weeks away and Wolfie... Well, he was here now.

Besides, it's not like she'd have to stick a thirty-five-pound bag of food up her dress. Her friend who worked for the pet supply store would happily put the supplies she needed aside so Sofia could pick them up after her shift.

Guilt gnawed at her gut. She'd always believed in making her own rules, but usually those rules merely raised a few eyebrows. They didn't break the law.

First, she'd committed a dog-napping, next up would be theft... What about after that?

No, she couldn't think like that. She was the hero here. She'd saved a dog's life, for crying out loud! So what if some billionaire CEO had a couple hundred bucks less in his pocket? *Boo freaking hoo.*

Yes, this is what she had to do, and she had to do it today before she left the mall. Once she rang out the lone customer in the store, Sofia picked up her phone and send a text to her friend, Blinky, who worked at Pets R Us. *Meet me for lunch in the food court at 12:30? I have a favor to ask.*

Having made up her mind now, the time, of course, dragged by. At least when Elizabeth Jane had still been working here, Sofia had someone to talk to. Ever since Liz had turned in her notice to go back to school and use her surprise inheritance to buy a horse ranch, Sofia had been left to work most of her shifts alone, turning her okay job into one she'd now come to loathe.

Their mall had undergone an expansion, complete with a new luxury department store and thus far fewer customers for their dinky chain boutique. Besides, who really went to the mall anymore? It was the twenty-first century. Normal human beings did their shopping at Amazon, eBay, or Etsy.

Heck, Sofia would never step foot in the place if it weren't for her job. She wished she had the discipline to live as a starving artist, but in the end, working for a soulless franchise would always be preferable to living on the streets... if only slightly.

When at last her lunch break rolled around, she temporarily shuttered the store and raced to the food court. She had less than a half an hour to herself, although the owner preferred she pack lunch and eat it in the back room rather than taking the legally mandated break.

It was hard to miss her friend, Blinky, who sat waiting for her in front of the A&W as he munched on fries and took long, slow sips from his root beer. "Sofi!" he said with a wave when he spotted her.

She hated when he called her that, but whatever. That wasn't what was important today. She needed a favor, and she needed it *bad*.

She plunked down into the chair across from her friend and stole a fistful of fries.

"Hey, get your own!" he said, batting her hand away before blinking three times hard. This was exactly why everyone called him "Blinky." His real name was Matt, but whenever he felt under pressure he developed this nervous tic where he'd—*you guessed it*—blink hard, fast, and a whole heck of a lot. And, apparently, Sofia stealing his fries warranted the twitch.

"I can't," she answered with a sigh. "I'm dead broke."

"Then why did you ask me to lunch? Miss me?" He puckered his lips at her and winked, which led to another fit of blinks.

"Sure, let's go with that." She had to fight back a groan. Blinky was so not her type. Sofia's type was the tall, inked, and handsome cop she'd met last night at the vet's office. As she liked to say, the forbidden fruit always tastes the best. She'd even gotten a tattoo to that effect.

Blinky teased her by plopping another fry into his mouth, letting a look of ecstasy cross his squinty features.

"Yeah, they're delicious," Sofia said, letting her groan out in full force. "Okay, you win. Look, I need a favor..."

Matt smiled as if he'd known all along Sofia needed his help with something crucial. Apparently he was the kind of friend who delighted in making others squirm. "I'm listening."

Sofia hated that she needed him as much as she did, but Wolfie was counting on her—and she refused to let him down.

# Five

After closing up her store for the night, Sofia met Blinky by the dumpsters behind the mall as he'd instructed.

"Hey," Blinky called, motioning her over with a noticeable lack of twitching. Apparently stealing was already second nature to him. Would it soon be for Sofia as well?

No, she wasn't a criminal—merely a woman providing for her dog by whatever means necessary.

"I thought you'd lose your nerve for sure." Her partner in crime looked her over with an approving gaze.

Sofia kicked at a broken hanger on the asphalt. "You thought I was joking? That I'd joke about something like this?"

"Not joking. Not exactly." He waited for her to look back up at him before saying, "I just always thought rebel was more of a fashion choice than a way of life for you."

"Har har." So, she was too different to fit in with the normies, but not different enough to belong to Blinky and his crew. *Lovely.*

Blinky scuttled behind the dumpster, talking to her as he worked to dislodge whatever he'd hidden back there. "Seems I underestimated you then. And, honestly, I like this version of Sofia Stepanov way better, anyway.

"Here you go." He pushed a box into her arms, then went back for more loot. And kept going back. The amount of contraband he'd set aside seemed like way too much for just one dog.

"Okay, that's everything," he said at last, dusting his hands off on the seat of his work-issued khakis.

"Great. Thanks for the help." Sofia turned to go, eager to be done with the actual act of stealing from Blinky's unwitting employer, but he stopped her by placing a firm hand on her shoulder.

"Look, I've got a meeting with my probation officer next week. I need to show him I'm working on turning my life around. That's what they expect, you know?" He shook his head and let out a soft chuckle. "Anyway, I sure could use a good outfit for that meeting."

Sofia's heart twisted in her chest. Everything came with a price. Of course. So why was she surprised that Blinky expected something in return for helping her? "When is it?"

Blinky dropped his hand from her shoulder, now that he had Sofia's full attention. "Next Tuesday."

She sighed, hating this. "I'm sorry... There's no way I have time to make you something that fast."

He laughed at her again, still no trace of his signature tick. "No, not *make*. Just borrow me something nice from your store."

She took a deep breath. Of course she'd known what he meant the moment he said it, but she still didn't want to believe it was true. "You want me to steal?" she asked for clarification.

Blinky continued to laugh at her. She'd never heard him laugh so much in all her life. Apparently, little fledgling criminal Sofia was a real hoot. "What do you think we're doing now, cupcake?"

"But that's different. I need this stuff for my dog, and I'll pay for it as soon as I get the chance."

He rolled his eyes and yanked the box away from her. "Yeah, and I need my new outfit. So, you want this stuff or not?"

"Fine." Sofia grabbed the box back from a laughing Blinky. "Just text me your sizes and I'll figure something out."

"Now that's more like it. Besides, one good favor deserves another, right?"

Sofia frowned. The stolen supplies felt unnaturally heavy within her outstretched arms. "I guess."

At last her friend's tic made itself known. He didn't speak until the blinks had worked themselves out. When he did, he seemed almost sorry, his voice kind and placating. "Don't look at me like that. You're the one who asked me to do this for you."

And it made her feel terribly guilty. "I know. I'm sorry. Thank you so much for the help. I'm just nervous, is all. This isn't something I normally do."

"It gets easier," he said with a conciliatory pat on her shoulder.

"I don't want it to get easier," Sofia said with a frustrated groan. "This is a one-time thing, remember?"

"Sure. Yes, of course." He hoisted up the large bag of dog food and carried it over to Sofia's car.

Once they'd packed all the supplies into her trunk, he turned to her and said, "Hey, listen, a bunch of us are hanging out at the Miners Pub Friday night. You should come on out. It's about time we took our friendship beyond the mall, don't you think?"

Guilt. Always with the guilt. She hated to say no, but she also hated the thought of saying yes. "I don't know. I have Wolfie now, and that's not really my scene, so..."

Blinky puckered his lips flirtatiously, laughing at her again. "If you're worried it's a date, it's not. My girlfriend will be there, too."

"Oh. Okay." That helped a little, but still, Sofia didn't really want to hang out with the kind of people who were okay with stealing. Even if she was suddenly becoming one of them.

Hope lit in his eyes. "So, you'll come?" he asked, slightly out of breath from the work of carrying the heavier supplies.

"I'll think about it," she promised.

Turned out she had a lot to think about these days. Too bad all this thinking wasn't providing any of the answers she needed.

# Six

Sofia drove home in a hurry. She'd left Wolfie alone in the apartment all day and had no idea what he could have done to keep himself busy during that time.

Sure, she'd considered closing him into the bathroom or confining him to the bedroom, but she hated the idea of locking him up when he'd only just secured his freedom. Still, the last thing she needed after the day she'd had was to come home to a scene straight out a disaster movie.

Hesitantly, she pushed open the door, calling out with a level voice as she did. "Wolfie? I'm home."

A joyous bark sounded from somewhere deep within the apartment, and a moment later her new pet appeared, wagging his tail furiously while sprinting toward her in a giant gray blur. He took a running leap and knocked her back into the doorframe, jumping and licking... and peeing everywhere.

"Ugh, Wolfie, gross!" Sofia shouted before she could remember that Wolfie didn't respond well to raised voices.

Back under the table he went, the peeing having intensified.

"Aww, boy. I'm sorry," she whispered. "I'm happy to see you, too. And, look, I brought you some cool stuff."

She found a dry patch of carpet and sat down so that Wolfie could watch as she unpacked the supplies Blinky had set aside for her. She hadn't noticed during their exchange at the dumpster, but apparently, Blinky had thought of everything. One by one she pulled out toys, chews, treats, and all matter of canine paraphernalia.

She offered Wolfie a stuffed duck toy with a squeaker inside, but he remained firmly ensconced beneath the table without so much as sniffing her offering. He didn't even budge when she opened up a bag of treats and held out a milk bone in her cupped palm.

Again, Sofia wanted to cry. She'd already risked so much for this dog and he didn't even care. "Oh, c'mon, Wolfie. I'm sorry I raised my voice. I missed you today. Come out and see me."

The dog made no move to join her.

"Please?" she begged.

Wolfie sighed as if she, too, was exasperating him.

"Fine, I guess I'll just make us some dinner." Sofia pushed herself up and returned to the hallway where she'd left the giant bag of large breed kibble. She peeled the sticker off the new metal dog dish from Blinky and then filled the bowl to the brim with smelly brown nibblets.

Wolfie remained uninterested, which meant Sofia was out of options. Why was he acting like this today? He'd been warmer toward her yesterday, when they hardly even knew each other. What had changed? Wasn't he happy to have been rescued?

So many questions, but none seemed to have answers she liked.

Maybe her friend, Elizabeth Jane, could help here. She'd grown up alongside many sled dogs, given that her father was a race officiant. And Wolfie was at least part sled dog. Could he really be part wolf, too, as Hunter had said?

The memory of Hunter's handsome smile drifted before her. Of course she had met the most attractive man in the whole world the same day she had committed her first serious crime in more than ten years.

*And he was a cop!*

Even if she hadn't stolen her dog, she still wouldn't be into the idea of dating someone so tied to the establishment. Yeah, maybe Blinky had thought she was a rebel by looks only, but Sofia had grown accustomed to living life on the periphery. No reason to change that now.

"Wolfie? Want some yummies?" she tried again, shaking the bowl at the still terrified dog.

"Okay, I'm calling Liz," she decided when the dog didn't react.

"Sofia. Everything okay?" her friend answered after three long rings.

"I'm not sure. He won't come out from under the table, and he won't eat."

"Yeah, that's the thing with rescues. You don't really know what their situations were like before you found them."

Sofia knew exactly what Wolfie's situation had been, but she couldn't tell Elizabeth Jane that.

Straight-laced Liz would demand Sofia turn Wolfie over to a shelter, and Sofia refused to do that. For better or for worse, she and this dog were an item now. And she was beginning to realize that she needed him every bit as much as he needed her.

"So, what should I do?" Sofia asked.

"I'm over at my old roommate Scarlett's apartment now. It's not too far from you, I think. See if Wolfie wants to go for a car ride. If he does, come on over. If he's used to roaming free, maybe he's just stressed about having been cooped up all day."

"Is that true, Wolfie?" Sofia said to the dog in a goochie-goo voice. "Want to go for a walk?"

Wolfie looked to the door, then back at Sofia.

She nodded vigorously. "Yes, a walk? Want to go outside?"

At last the dog yawned, stretched, and then stepped out from under the table.

"Oh, that worked," Sofia announced, making sure to keep her voice neutral so as not to scare the poor dog again. "I guess we're coming over."

"Great! Can't wait to see you!" Liz cooed before hanging up the phone. Although she hadn't had time for Sofia yesterday, she seemed to be bending over backward to help today.

Well, Sofia would take whatever help she could get. Her evening with Blinky had proven that.

"What is it about you that always gets me into trouble?" she asked Wolfie as they charged down the apartment stairs.

Of course, he did not have an answer for her.

# Seven

Riding in the car, Wolfie became a completely different dog. He panted happily and shifted from one side of the seat to the other, back and forth. It seemed he was afraid of missing even a single thing on their journey.

Sofia laughed and rolled down the windows so he could stick his head through and sniff the crisp Anchorage air.

Luckily for the happy canine, Scarlett's apartment lay on the other, nicer side of town, which made their journey a lengthy one. When at last they arrived, Wolfie sobered up, following her calmly into the new building—the perfect picture of canine obedience. He sure liked to keep her guessing.

"Whoa, big dog," Elizabeth Jane clucked when

she took in the sight of Wolfie at the doorway. He hadn't seemed that big to Sofia, but when she saw him beside Scarlett's two huskies, Fantine and Cosette, the size difference became very, very obvious.

"He's almost as big as Fred," Scarlett pointed out with a smile, then explained, "Fred was my wheel dog when I ran the Iditarod a couple years back. He's still on Lauren Ramsey's team to this day. Hey, do you know Lauren?"

"I don't keep up with the races." Sofia shook her head. "I mean, I'm not really a dog person."

"Looks like you are now." Elizabeth Jane laughed and gave Sofia a hug hello. Sofia had never been a hugger, but she'd learned to grin and bear it with Liz.

"What can you tell us about him?" Scarlett asked at the same time Wolfie and her dogs struck up a wrestling match in the middle of the living room floor, complete with play growls and flying fur.

Wolfie's growls sounded different than those of the huskies. Would he accidentally hurt the two smaller dogs? Neither Liz nor Scarlett said anything, so Sofia did her best to swallow down her worry and focus on their conversation.

She'd practiced Wolfie's origin story on the way over and repeated the exact words she'd prepared for the occasion. "I found him walking along the side of the road. When I opened my door, he jumped right in. He gets scared easily and likes to hide under the table. He also pees. A lot. But not a single drop of it has been outside."

Now Scarlett's face twisted with concern. She bit her lip, then asked, "Are you sure he was ever a pet?"

Sofia shrugged, thinking back to her first glimpse of Wolfie chained out in some shanty's front yard. "Maybe. Maybe not. But he *is* my pet now, and I want to do right by him."

"Well, I'm pretty sure he's not a pure wolf," Elizabeth Jane said as she appraised Wolfie from across the room. "But he's not a pure husky, either."

"Actually, he might be part Malamute," Scarlett argued. "It would explain the size. And why he reminds me so much of Fred."

Sofia remembered what the cute cop at the vet's office had said about wolf hybrids being illegal. She had hoped he was wrong about Wolfie, but apparently Scarlett and Elizabeth Jane saw it, too. She gulped. "Why does his breed matter? Isn't every dog its own person?"

"Well, yes and no. If he's a wolf hybrid, then that kind of changes everything." Scarlett's eyes widened, and she looked to Elizabeth Jane before speaking again. "Keeping a wolf hybrid as a pet is super illegal in Alaska."

"You can't be serious?" Sofia feigned shock. At this point, her rap sheet was getting to be as long as a CVS receipt.

Liz gulped and shook her head. "Afraid so."

"Well, who said anything about a wolf hybrid? He's a sled dog mutt. Malamute, you said?"

Scarlett sighed. "Yeah, but—"

"But *nothing*. He's had a tough life, and I'm not abandoning him, so forget anything about wolf hybrids."

"But you're the one who named him Wolfie," Scarlett said, hardly above a whisper.

Sofia had only just met Elizabeth Jane's former roommate, but already she didn't much care for her. She'd come to her friend and former employee for help, and she really didn't need this wispy blonde girl judging her about it.

"Yeah, because he reminded me of the Three Little Pigs and Little Red Riding Hood," she snapped, giving Scarlett a pointed gaze. "Not because I honestly thought he was part White Fang."

Scarlett twisted her hands in her lap and bit her lip again. "If you're sure..."

Sofia glanced toward Elizabeth Jane. Why wasn't

their supposed friend helping either of them? Where was her head at today?

Elizabeth Jane kept her eyes glued to the floor, leaving Sofia to fight for her own honor.

"I'm sure," she said with what she hoped was a peace-keeping smile. "Now do you have any idea what I can do about all the peeing and hiding under the table?"

Sofia nodded as Scarlett gave her loads of advice and even texted her links to different web articles on separation anxiety, obedience training, and pack dynamics. Liz pitched in advice occasionally, but clearly, she was distracted by something she didn't feel comfortable sharing with the others.

Or at least with Sofia.

Had she interrupted something important between Scarlett and Elizabeth Jane? And, if so, what was it?

Suddenly, Sofia felt incredibly alone.

# Eight

Sofia stayed for a late dinner at Scarlett's insistence. Even though the two friends of Elizabeth Jane had eventually started to warm to each other, Sofia was more than ready to head home and crawl into bed.

Wolfie, for his part, seemed to enjoy the company of the two huskies. Scarlett even gave them a standing invite for a doggie playdate whenever Sofia and Wolfie wanted to drop by for a visit.

Sofia appreciated the help but—between work, Blinky, and now this visit—she'd already had more than enough extroverting for the week.

Unfortunately, fate had other ideas as Sofia headed out of the building and into the night. A thud sounded from across the parking lot, which set

Wolfie on the defensive. And when a woman appeared from around the dumpster, he raised the ridge of hairs on his back and let out a low growl.

"It's okay, boy. It's okay. C'mon," Sofia urged, trying to direct him the rest of the way toward her car, but Wolfie remained rooted to the spot, his eyes fixed narrowly at the woman as she approached them.

*Oh, please don't attack this person,* Sofia prayed.

"Sofia Stepanov, is that you?" the woman asked in an unsettlingly familiar voice, as she moved in front of a street lamp, illuminating her auburn hair and delicate features.

*Crap.* Sofia knew exactly who stood before her now, and it was someone she had hoped she'd never meet another day in her life. "Hi, Celeste," she murmured.

"Oh my gosh!" Celeste cried, raising both hands to cover her mouth, even though presumably she'd just been handling garbage. "It is you! Look at you, all grown up!"

Sofia rolled her eyes as she'd always done when dealing with the former teen queen. There were few people in the world Sofia liked less than Celeste Lyons, especially now that coming face-to-face with the woman sent a tremendous wave of guilt rippling through her core.

Sofia shook her head and did her best not to frown. "Yes, I'm a grown-up now."

"You haven't changed one bit," Celeste exclaimed with the shimmer of fresh tears in her cornflower blue eyes.

*Have you?* Sofia wanted to ask. *Did you learn anything since high school?*

These questions were meant to be rhetorical, which meant Sofia definitely wasn't expecting what came next.

Celeste let out a dramatic sigh and released a torrent of tears that seemed like they might even be real. "Sofia, I'm really glad I ran into you, because I want to tell you how sorry I am for… well, everything Allie and I did to you. We were just stupid kids, you know?"

Sofia waved her off, but Celeste kept rambling on anyway.

*Please stop*, Sofia thought on loop, trying to drown out Celeste's apology. She didn't want to remember what they had done to her… or what she had done to them. Of course, Celeste had no idea she had ever taken her revenge, or that it had changed the course of her life so much. With any luck, she would never know.

Celeste sniffed and wiped at her eyes as if the memories were now causing her physical pain. "No, really. We were just awful to you. Nobody deserves to be treated that way. Could you ever forgive us? Forgive me?"

"Water under the bridge," Sofia said without meeting her eyes.

Wolfie growled beside her.

Celeste's entire face lit up with joy. No wonder she'd been the lead in the school play every year since kindergarten. "Do you mean it? Really? Oh, thank you so much. You have no idea what a weight off my chest this is."

Sofia glanced toward Celeste's barely-there chest area and swallowed back the sarcastic comment beginning to form in her throat. One of the reasons the other students had teased Sofia mercilessly was due to her early and ample bosom development. Well, the joke was on them. Sofia now filled out a dress wonderfully, and Celeste had never crossed the line between a B and C cup.

"Yeah, okay. Well, I have to get him home," Sofia said politely, gesturing toward Wolfie, who was still noticeably upset by the presence of Sofia's former bully.

"Oh, sure. Right. Can we..." Celeste glanced around the parking lot before continuing. "Can we meet sometime? Maybe catch up?"

"Yeah, yeah, I'll see you around." Sofia tightened her grip on Wolfie's leash and hurried as fast as she could toward her car without actually running.

"Okay, you've got my attention," she muttered to God as she jammed her key into the ignition. "But I have no idea what you're trying to say."

# Nine

S ofia called in sick to work the next day. A gnawing feeling had developed in her gut from the moment she'd first liberated Wolfie from his chains—and seeing Celeste the night before had kicked it up several notches.

There was no way she could play nice with preppy mall moms and their tweens today. No, she needed some time to get her head on straight, to remember all the things she loved in life, and to remind herself that—*yes*—she'd done a bad thing, but she'd done it for all the right reasons.

And the best way to find her center would undoubtedly be to feel the thread between her fingers, to bring simple parts together to create something wonderful.

Fashion proved to be both predictable and unpredictable at the same time, and she needed that now. If you followed your pattern and took all the right steps, you'd end up with a completed garment every single time. But the range of possibilities was also endless. She could just as easily create a ball gown as she could a cocktail dress. Or a business suit.

Through fashion, she could help others see her the way she saw herself. Sofia could also change how she felt inside. A little satin, a few buttons, and a whole lot of confidence.

It was like magic.

She'd been so proud of the first dress she'd made by her own hands. Over Christmas break one year, her grandmother had shown her how to work the old Singer sewing machine and given her a pattern to follow. While the seams were a little loose in some places and the hemline more than a little uneven, Sofia had never seen a nicer garment in all her life.

It was intoxicating, weaving all the separate parts together to make a new whole. In a way it meant that anything could be reshaped, restructured, reinvigorated, if only you had a little thread and time.

She liked that then, and she *lived by it* now.

Sewing would clear her mind, return her to herself.

Yes, when taken individually, she'd committed a few small crimes over the past week. But put them together? She'd saved a life, and that felt pretty darn great.

Each day Wolfie seemed to trust her more, peed on her less, and generally began to treat her like a partner and friend.

Sofia and Wolfie against the world, for better or worse.

Happily ever after.

Yes, she'd always fancied herself a fairytale character, but she generally related more to the ugly step-sister or the placeholder best friend, the girl who got cast aside when the real heroine made her appearance.

Now with Wolfie at her side, she felt strong, brave, worthy.

She'd contributed something positive to the world in saving him. No, she wasn't as selfish as her father had always claimed. She'd taken risks, and she hadn't even wanted a dog—let alone one that was part wild animal.

Seeing Wolfie raise his hackles to defend her last night, though, proved that the risks she'd taken to help him had been well worth it. This dog understood her. Somehow he knew Celeste was not a friend, and he warned her away.

Just like that.

Sofia didn't have to say a word. If only people could be like that.

As she worked on the neckline for a new blouse, she thought back to the first time she'd looked into Wolfie's amber eyes.

He'd seen her then, but she saw him now, too.

And she would do whatever it took to keep him safe and to keep him with her, illegal or not. Some things were above the law.

Like love. Like friendship.

Power coursed through Sofia's veins as she worked the pedal under her foot. She'd made a difference. She'd done something huge. Which meant she could do it again. She could change her life if she wanted to.

Like those fairytale princesses, she only had to believe it in her heart.

No more dead-end retail job. She'd taken one risk and now it was time to take another. To believe in herself and her fashions. To do what she loved for real—for a living.

Blinky had said he assumed rebel was a fashion choice for her. Maybe it would be a fashion choice for others, too. She loved the flowy skirts and bright patterns of retro fashion. What would it look like to marry them with the sharp lines and bold insignias well-loved by rebels the world over?

Yes, that was the direction she needed. Something new and fresh. A whole new line to make her mark on the world, to clothe even more strangers, to help them feel the confidence she felt now.

*Vigilante.*

That's what she'd become when she rescued Wolfie that day, and now that was what she'd call her new fashion line.

Sometimes people just had to take matters into their own hands, to make their own way. A vigilante was even better than a rebel, because vigilantes got things done. Just like Sofia would get things done, first by prepping her new fashion line and then by making a living doing what she was born to do.

All with her living spirit animal—*with Wolfie*—right by her side.

# Ten

*re you coming?*

    The text from Blinky lit up Sofia's phone. She hadn't planned on meeting Blinky and his friends at the Miners Pub, but she also hadn't planned on having a three-day stroke of creative fury for her new fashion line.

Her first custom Vigilante dress was all stitched up with no place to go.

Sofia took a moment to eye the knee-length frock with the sweetheart neckline and belle sleeves. Normally she preferred to stick to a stark black pallet, but for this special garment, she'd ventured slightly out of her comfort zone, crafting the dress with a stunning sapphire blue. The bell-shaped sleeves hid little bursts of candy apple red that were only visible when she lifted or waved her arms. The undercarriage of the skirt was also lined with red tulle, so that if she found herself having a Marilyn Monroe moment, all eyes would be on the dress and not her bright yellow underwear beneath.

She'd recently dyed the ends of her hair a matching red, which completed the look perfectly. And all her best tattoos were visible, too—including her newest, a watercolor design sporting a snake wrapped around an apple.

The forbidden fruit.

It would be a shame to keep this gorgeous new ensemble hidden in the bowels of her closet. Visiting Blinky and his friends for a few hours was just as good an excuse as any to take it out for a spin.

And, really, what could it hurt getting to know one of her work friends outside of the mall? Sofia had finally forgiven herself for obtaining Wolfie and the supplies needed to take care of him by less than legal means. She'd cooled off from her weird encounter with Celeste, too.

The weekend had arrived, and she may as well put on her best party dress to go shoot some pool with Blinky and whatever ragtag band of friends he'd managed to acquire on his few hours spent outside of Pets R Us.

Sofia didn't get out enough, either. Maybe it was time to change all that.

Maybe tonight would be the start of something new and wonderful.

Maybe, maybe...

*Yes,* she texted back. *I'll be there. What time?*

Wolfie whined and stuck his face between his paws as he watched Sofia get ready. He'd been her only company these last couple days and had apparently gotten used to the sight of her in pajamas with her hand mussed up and no bra or makeup.

"Aww, Wolf," Sofia tutted. "I'll be back before you know it."

Wolfie let out another sharp whine and anxiously pawed at the carpet.

Sofia puckered her lips and applied a fresh coat of her favorite lipstick. "How about I bring you a hotdog when I come back? Yeah? You want a hotdog?"

Her canine companion lifted his head tentatively and thumped his tail three times before falling back into his previous position.

Sofia laughed. "You drive a tough bargain. Okay, *two* hotdogs!" She waved her fingers as if talking to a toddler and not a too-intelligent-for-his-own-good wolf hybrid.

Wolfie barked and licked a trail of slime up Sofia's bare leg.

"Hey, now we're spit buddies," she joked, patting Wolfie's head playfully as she thought back to all the summers she'd spent at music camp with plenty of time to practice her oboe, but very few friends to keep her company outside of recitals.

This was ridiculous.

Sofia was a grown-up. She had friends who wanted to spend time with her. She'd become a talented—albeit struggling—fashion designer. Yeah, she'd come a long way from that lonely twelve-year-old girl, a long way from that angry teen who would do anything to get even with her tormentors...

"No, mustn't think like that!" she sang to Wolfie, grabbing her keys and a small clutch before floating out through the door. "TTFN!"

# Eleven

⌒∽⌒

Walking into the Miners Pub felt like a scene straight out of a movie. It wasn't that everyone's eyes snapped to the doorway where Sofia stood backlit like some kind of barroom angel, because that definitely didn't happen. Actually, only one person seemed to notice her arrival at all, but when he did, his eyes locked onto her, pulling her toward him like a fish on the line.

"So we meet again," the handsome dog-owning police officer, Hunter, said with a bright, shining grin that made Sofia wilt beneath the heat of his gaze.

Sofia nodded. "Hi," she managed, taken once again by just how perfect everything about this man seemed. Well, everything except for the fact that he was a cop and that she had committed at least three crimes in the past week.

Hunter kicked back the chair next to him in one fluid motion. "Have a seat and tell me what you're drinking. It's on me."

She climbed up onto the seat cautiously, careful to arrange her dress in a way that wouldn't wrinkle or show off too much skin. "I don't drink, actually."

Hunter stared at her blankly for a few horrible seconds, then broke out into a smile. "Of course, of course. One Shirley Temple it is." He motioned for the bartender and gave him an order for two non-alcoholic drinks.

"Thank you," she murmured. Would it be rude to rush off and find her friends the moment the drink arrived? Or would it be worse to blow off Blinky and spend the rest of the night with Hunter, pretending they could ever be a thing? Somehow, she didn't anticipate the two very different men getting along, so then why did she like them both—Blinky as a friend, and Hunter as...?

No, that wasn't going to happen. Couldn't happen. Sofia shifted in her chair and glanced around the bar, plotting her escape.

Hunter put a hand on the back of her chair and turned his whole body into hers. "So, what's a pretty girl like you doing in a rundown place like this?" The end of his sentence broke apart in laughter.

"Sorry, sorry," he said. "I've always wanted to say that, but now that I have, I hear how ridiculous I sound."

Sofia smiled politely, then searched Hunter's arms, hoping the partially hidden tattoo she'd noticed at the vet's office would be fully visible.

He caught her eye and rolled up his sleeve. "It's Japanese. Means *honor bound*." Of course. Kanji tattoos were as basic as they came, but still, the design looked good on him.

"I like yours, too," he said, nodding toward Sofia's chest, a slight pink hue rising to the apples of his cheeks. "The Garden of Eden?"

"It's the forbidden fruit. I have twelve others, too."

"Forbidden?" Hunter stroked the scruff on his chin as the bartender set their pair of mocktails before them.

"*Fruit*," Sofia finished for him, feeling like a moron.

Hunter chuckled. "I like it."

Sofia took a delicate sip of her drink, enjoying the taste of grenadine on her tongue. Normally she wasn't the delicate type, but Hunter kept her on her tiptoes. After their first meeting, she'd thought he was just another police flunky, but he seemed different tonight. And he definitely liked Sofia despite her "rebel as a fashion choice" style.

This left her equal parts excited and confused. She couldn't start something with Hunter, though she did like that she had the option should her judgment—or her willpower—lapse unexpectedly.

"So, tell me." Hunter leaned in close as if to reveal a long-awaited secret. Her head spun as he drew nearer. If Sofia were a superhero, then Hunter would definitely be her Kryptonite. Something about this man just got under her skin and made her tingle all over.

"Why didn't you call?" he whispered in a breathy growl.

Her focus drew to his lips, and it took Sofia a moment to realize what he had said. "What? Oh. I..."

He smiled and shifted back in his chair to face the bar. "Relax, I'm just giving you a hard time."

The tension in the air dissipated somewhat as Hunter put those few precious inches back between them. Still, Sofia didn't know what to say, so she said nothing.

"Maybe this time you could give me your

number," he suggested with a quick shrug and a lingering grin.

Sofia panicked. She couldn't see any way out of this one, and she hated to start a relationship on lies —such as letting Hunter believe she wasn't a criminal. Then again, her heart raced for him. Sofia had never been one for clichés, but she'd also never felt the first pinpricks of love.

She was so royally screwed. Unable to avoid it— to avoid him—any longer, she took a deep breath and opened her mouth to speak. "I—"

"Hey, there you are!" Blinky rushed up behind her and leaned over the counter. "I was beginning to think you stood us up, Sofi."

"Sofia?" Hunter asked with a pointed gaze, perhaps awaiting her number, perhaps an introduction. She would give him neither.

Blinky looked over to the other man and broke into a nervous fit. His composure remained relaxed and easy, but the rapid contortion of his face clearly revealed his anxiety.

"Gotta go. Nice seeing you again." She leaned forward and offered Hunter a quick kiss on the cheek, emboldened by the fact that she now had a way to escape. "Thank you for the drink."

"C'mon, c'mon." Blinky grabbed her by the arm and pulled. "Lots of people for you to meet."

When Sofia glanced back at Hunter, he seemed more than a little confused.

*Yeah. Me too*, she thought. *Me too.*

## Twelve

ofia followed Blinky over to the corner of the pub where three dilapidated pool tables stood in a slightly crooked row. Six people crowded around the edges of the farthest table, and Blinky pulled her right over to them.

"I'm racking up. Who's in?" the tallest one said as he eyed Sofia suspiciously.

She felt trapped beneath his gaze, unable to look away herself as she watched the overhead lighting reflect off his cue-ball scalp. He could have been handsome if not for his oversized ears, which protruded uncomfortably far from his bare head. One of his arms was covered to the wrist in a full sleeve of colorful tattoos, while the other was totally bare. Both were long and thin, accented by oversized hands.

Blinky jabbed her in the ribs and whispered in her ear, "That's the D-Man. He's your date."

"What? Oh, no, no, no, no, no, *no*." Sofia took a step back, her chest tightening with a sudden spike of anxiety. Was it too late to hightail it the heck out of there?

Blinky took a swig of the beer bottle he held by the neck. The label had been peeled off messily, leaving a sticky residue behind. "Hey, D-Man! Come over here for a sec!"

"What are you doing?" Sofia growled as quietly as she could despite her growing anger at having been set up.

At that moment, she desperately wished she'd somehow managed to smuggle Wolfie into the bar with her. He would have put a stop to this—defended her like he did with Celeste.

"It's fine. You're fine," Blinky whispered to her before hooking his arm around D-Man's shoulders and pulling him over. His eyes danced with mischief as he made their official introduction. "This is the girl I told you about. Sofi."

"Hi, Sofi," D-Man said with a half-hearted wave. His shy blush overtook not just his cheeks, but his entire head. She probably *would* like him if it weren't for Blinky's ill-advised matchmaking.

"Umm, hi, D... M-Man." She felt ridiculous for calling him by the stupid nickname when she hardly even knew him. What if the *D* was for something scandalous? She didn't want any part of that, thanks.

He laughed good-naturedly, putting Sofia slightly more at ease. "The D is for Dope."

"Because you're so cool?" Sofia laughed, too. Even if Blinky was being rude tonight, at least D-Man had the good sense to treat her like a gentleman.

Blinky hooked an arm around each of them and pulled their small group into an awkwardly intimate huddle. "No, because he's our supplier. If you ever need anything, D-Man is your guy."

"I'll keep that in mind," Sofia said as she wriggled away. "Umm, can you introduce me to the others?"

D-Man's face fell for a brief moment before he rearranged it back into a placating grin. Sofia didn't know what Blinky had told him about her or what he had promised about tonight, and she suspected it would be better if she never knew.

Blinky shoved the two of them together again, then traveled from one friend to the next. Each had a ridiculous nickname, making her think she'd gotten off easy seeing as he'd only dropped the last syllable from her name. Sure, *Sofi* wasn't her first choice in nicknames, but it beat being called any of these other things.

"And this is Pretty." Blinky introduced the final member of his friend circle by crushing his lips to hers in an over-the-top display of public affection.

"It's Preeti, actually," the woman explained once Blinky had pried his face off hers. "You can call me that if it's easier."

"Preeti," Sofia repeated.

"It's Indian. My parents are second generation, I don't know why they couldn't have given me a more normal name, but whatever."

"Hey! I love your name, babe." Blinky claimed Preeti again with a sickening display of teenage-like saliva swapping.

"Yeah, they're always like that," D-Man said softly beside her. "And, yes, they're trying to set us up. If you haven't noticed, everyone else is coupled up, and they're sick of me being the odd man out."

Not this again. How many times did she have to say no before it would stick? "That's really nice of them, but—"

"Relax, I can tell you're not interested. And you're very beautiful and everything, but I'm not interested either. Besides, that guy over there hasn't been able to take his eyes off you all night."

Sofia's eyes shot back to the bar, where—sure enough—Hunter sat watching her with a bemused smirk.

"Thanks, D-Ma—" She stopped and shook her head. "Is there something else I could call you?"

D-Man laughed and pointed to one of his tattoos.

Sofia squinted to read the small tattoo in the poor light of the pub. "Matt?"

"Yup. That's why the nicknames started. Not that you could really confuse me and Blinky for the same guy, but anyway... You should go talk to that guy. It looks like he has something to say."

"Thanks for understanding," Sofia said. "I'll be back in a few minutes."

She took a deep breath before turning toward the bar, once again drawn in like a fish on the line. What was it about Hunter that affected her so?

And how could she make it go away?

# Thirteen

"Why are you staring at me?" Sofia demanded after marching straight up to Hunter and slamming her hand down onto the bar in front of him.

He shrugged, completely unfazed. "Why not?"

"Really?" She shifted her weight and crossed her arms over her chest. "*That's* your explanation?"

He took a slow sip from his drink before answering. "Okay, okay. I was just measuring up the competition."

"What? D-Man? *No.*" Sofia looked back toward the group. They'd already moved on to their next game of pool. D-Man caught her eye and waved, bringing a fresh wave of guilt bubbling to the surface. She'd summarily rejected him without giving

71

it even a second's worth of thought. Was she being unfair?

Then again, he was a drug dealer—not exactly the top of Sofia's list when it came to potential boyfriends.

Still, neither was a cop like Hunter. And yet...

A grin of satisfaction crossed his face, almost as if he knew the exact effect he was having on Sofia—and relished in it. "So I've got you all to myself then?"

"I didn't say..." She stomped her foot, making her skirt swish across her knees with a soft tickle. "You're infuriating. You know that?"

"I can see I have that effect on you." Another slow sip, a raise of his eyebrow, an entirely too self-assured demeanor.

She sighed and waited for him to finish his drink before asking, "Look, if I give you my number, will you let me enjoy my night?"

Hunter wiped his lips with the back of his hand, drawing Sofia's eyes once again to the last place she needed to be looking. "No can do," he said before winking at her as if they shared some unspoken secret. "Besides, it didn't really look like you were enjoying yourself all that much anyway."

She looked back at the group again, then turned to Hunter, hoping her irritation came through loud and clear. "How would you even know that? You've known me for a grand total of, like, ten minutes."

A roar of thunder sounded above, so loud they both heard it over the music and din of the bar. Not a second later, a torrent of rain pounded down on the roof, creating a steady background melody to their conversation.

They both looked up and then at each other before Hunter picked up their conversation from the exact point they'd left it.

"Detective skills." He winked at her again and made an odd clicking sound that might have resembled cocking a gun. Sofia had never held a gun a day in her life, so she really couldn't be sure. "They don't pay me the big bucks for nothing. By the way, did you know I've picked up that guy with Tourette's at least a half dozen times for petty theft?"

"That's none of my business." Sofia flushed at the mention of Blinky's crimes, especially since she'd been an accessory to them at least once. "What I want to know is why you insist on bothering me."

Hunter turned in his seat and brought the full force of his gaze directly to Sofia. "Am I?" he asked.

"Yes... No... *Grr*, I don't know!" For the second time that night, she wished Wolfie was at her side. Maybe that was why she'd channeled him in her response. For the time being, unfortunately, Hunter was her problem and hers alone.

"You want my number, right? *Here.*" She grabbed a lipstick from her clutch and wrote her digits on a fresh napkin from the stack at the end of the bar.

"Oooh, sexy," Hunter said as he accepted the napkin with what she now thought of as his signature smirk.

"I'm mad at you now." She pouted. "That was my favorite lipstick."

He laughed, tucking the napkin into the breast pocket of his button-up flannel. "You could have asked for a pen, or for my phone."

Yeah, that's what she should have done, but she couldn't think straight when Hunter was around. Yet another reason she needed to get out of there ASAP. "Are we done here now?" she demanded.

He shook his head before rising to his feet to stand intoxicatingly close. "No, not yet."

"Then?" Sofia widened her eyes and let out a little huff. She just couldn't win with this guy.

Hunter placed one hand at the edge of the bar. His arm was so close to hers that even a slight shiver would cause them to touch.

"Now you have to agree to meet me for a date," he said.

A little thrill shot up Sofia's spine and—sure enough—the extra little jolt was just enough to make her skin connect with Hunter's. Why did he have this effect on her? And why didn't she just walk away? She didn't owe him anything, but still she couldn't escape—didn't want to, either.

"You said you only wanted my number."

He moved his hand further down the bar, bringing more of their skin into contact. How come the feel of his arm against hers was a million times better than any first kiss Sofia had ever had? And if being close to Hunter was this good, what *would* it be like to kiss him?

He smiled slowly. Oh, he knew how much torment this caused her—and he obviously liked it. "Yeah, but you blew me off, so I've upped the stakes."

Another knife of thunder sliced through the air unseen, and Sofia gulped. "The stakes? What is this? A game of poker?"

"It kind of feels that way with you. So, hey, let me lay all my cards out there, then you'll know I'm not bluffing. I like you. I want to get to know you better." He slid closer still.

Sofia winced from equal parts pleasure and pain. "Why?"

"Why not?" Hunter slipped his hand onto hers, lighting a blaze within her.

"You really know how to charm a girl." She rolled her eyes, hoping the sudden sarcasm would throw him off the scent, would hide how much she enjoyed being near him.

He frowned. "Not enough?"

Sofia shook her head and, despite her best efforts, a little smile slipped through.

"Well, you're gorgeous for starters," Hunter said without the least bit of hesitation, squeezing her hand in his now. "And somehow you manage to be both shy and sassy at the same time. I already know you're a dog person, which gets you major points."

"That all?" she sputtered. Normally, words were easy to find, but not with Hunter.

He chuckled. "Well, I've only known you for a grand total of like..." He swiped at his phone to revive the screen. "Fourteen minutes now? But I'm willing to bet there's a lot more I'd like about you, which is why I want you to meet me for a date."

She glanced around the bar, her eyes locking momentarily with Blinky's before she turned back to Hunter. "Where? Here?"

"Yeah, *no*." Hunter looked genuinely offended by this assertion. "What do you take me for? We'd go somewhere much nicer."

"Like?" Sweat began to bead on Sofia's palm. She needed to end this.

"It will be a surprise," Hunter promised with an optimistic grin.

"A surprise, meaning you haven't figured it out yet. Maybe because you know I'm not planning on saying yes." She yanked her hand away from his and folded both arms across her chest. Hopefully the physical shield would help to put her guard back up.

Hunter laughed, unperturbed by this small rejection. "First off, you're dying to say yes. Secondly, I have the perfect place in mind, but I like to lead with a bit of mystery. Basically, you'll have to agree to go out with me in order to find out."

Sofia shivered again. "You drive a tough bargain, Mr. Burke."

"Remembered my last name, did you?"

Sofia's breath felt stuck in her chest. "So what?"

"But you don't like me," he said flatly. "Yeah, I'm not buying it."

The more time she spent in Hunter's company, the more deeply she fell under his spell. At this point, there was no way she could win. She needed to go before she unwittingly accepted a second date or a marriage proposal.

"Fine. I'll go out with you," she said with more confidence than she felt before turning back toward the billiard tables and shouting the rest over her shoulder. "Text me the details. You have my number."

# Fourteen

∽

After she'd finally caved and accepted Hunter's request for a date, Sofia returned to Blinky and his friends at the pool tables. Not long after, Hunter disappeared from the bar, which meant she could finally allow herself to relax and enjoy her night out.

"I love your dress and your hair and your lipstick," Preeti gushed as she ran her hands across the fabric on Sofia's sleeves and then dug her fingers into her hair. "I should have you give me a makeover," she concluded with a smile that didn't seem entirely genuine. Still, at least she was making an effort to be nice. Most of the others—including Blinky—had decided to largely ignore her after she vetoed their ambush matchmaking.

Sofia tried to picture herself doing girl things with Preeti. Other than their mutual acquaintance of Blinky, they seemed to have little in common, but Sofia rarely felt like she could relate to new people, so maybe she was already being too hard on the girl.

She smiled, hoping her gesture would appear more authentic than Preeti's. She hated being fake, but she hated being mean, too. "I could, if that's what you want," she offered. "I actually design my own clothes. I could make something for you, too."

Preeti waved Sofia's suggestion off. "Nah, that sounds way too expensive. I'll figure something else out."

*But what?* Sofia wondered darkly.

After all, she already knew Blinky shoplifted, and that D-Man dealt drugs. Did everyone in the group regularly engage in some kind of crime? And if so, what was Preeti's? Sofia wanted to ask her, but that hardly felt like small talk.

After playing two rounds on the winning team and two rounds for the losing team, Sofia decided to call it a night. Everyone else was already pretty intoxicated and she felt like the odd one out staying sober.

D-Man saddled her with a hug, squeezing her tight. "I hope to see you again. Give us a chance. We're not so bad."

"I believe you," Sofia wheezed, then laughed when he finally let her go. "I'm sure I'll be seeing you soon."

She punched her number into D-Man's and Preeti's phones before heading out into the pouring rain. She half expected to find Hunter waiting for her under the awning, but she remained blissfully alone in the half empty parking lot.

By the time she reached the safety of her car, Sofia's gorgeous new dress had soaked through to its very core. She shivered and sent up a prayer that the car's antiquated heater would do its job just a little bit faster.

Although the wipers swished back and forth at the highest setting, she could barely see the road before her as she pulled away from Miners Pub. It was by pure luck she noticed the fat Chow Chow pacing the fence not two blocks from the neighborhood where she had first found Wolfie. The rain let up for a brief moment, but still, it was long enough for Sofia to make an important decision.

Knowing it was a risk, she pulled up to the curb just outside of the house, determined to make another quick rescue. This dog needed someone to save it—and since nobody else was around, that job just fell to Sofia.

She rushed through the rain to open the back door of her car, then unlatched the gate and called to the drenched dog.

And the Chow Chow knew just what to do. She raced from her yard and hopped straight into Sofia's car with a joyous bark.

"Good dog," Sofia muttered as she slammed the door behind her, then peeled away as fast as the rain would allow.

And just like that, she had acquired a second dog in less than a week's time.

Wolfie had needed her help, and this dog had, too. Rain had been pounding down from the Anchorage sky all evening. Who would leave their dog out in such a horrible storm? Not anyone who deserved the privilege of caring for such a magnificent creature.

Sofia placed one hand in front of the heater in her dashboard, then the other.

"Your face is smushed in, but you kind of look like a fox," she told the Chow Chow while waiting for the stoplight to turn. "I'll call you Foxie."

Foxie answered by giving her coat a good shake and sending water droplets shooting in every direction. The moment she finished, she climbed over the hump and into the front seat with Sofia.

"Well, aren't you a lovey thing," she said with a laugh as Foxie licked her in the face.

And this time she didn't even feel guilty about doing what had needed to be done.

# *Fifteen*

S ofia found she didn't even need a leash for Foxie. The bedraggled orange dog followed her right into the house with minimal prompting on her part.

Even before she opened the door to her apartment, she heard Wolfie's boisterous barking on the other side. He had missed her that night, which made her feel guilty, but at least she'd brought him a new friend so that he wouldn't be so lonely the next time she had to leave.

The Chow pushed through the door before Sofia could even finish opening it all the way, and when Wolfie came running over to say hello, Foxie bared her teeth, which sent him skittering beneath the table.

"Hey, hey, none of that," Sofia warned, leaving the dogs briefly to fetch an old beach towel from the linen closet. When she returned, she found Foxie with her head under the table and both dogs growling.

"Stop, stop! No fighting!" she cried.

The sound of her raised voice made Wolfie pee—because apparently an angry human was infinitely scarier than an attacking dog.

Foxie let out one more warning woof, then extracted herself from beneath the table and licked Sofia's arm as if to officially stake her claim over their resident caretaker.

"Maybe this isn't going to work quite as well as I thought," Sofia mumbled while wicking moisture from the Chow Chow's coat.

Wolfie whined from his spot under the table, and Foxie jerked loose from Sofia's grasp to dive in after him. The chairs fell back like the opening of a Venus fly trap, the two big dogs tangled in battle at the center.

"Stop! Stop! Stop!" Sofia could barely hear her own cries as the dogs' growling graduated to full-on snarling.

Wolfie let out a sharp yelp of pain, but Sofia couldn't see what had happened in their arena beneath the dining room table. She desperately wished she could stop the fight but didn't know how to without risking getting accidentally bitten herself.

Somehow she needed to lure them out and get them separated. Only one idea sprung to mind—hopefully it would work.

After charging into the kitchen, Sofia grabbed a Styrofoam container of leftover kung pao chicken and opened it as quick as her shaking fingers would allow.

"Want some?" she called to the dogs as pulled out a big hunk of meat and held it high in the air.

Immediately Foxie came trotting over as if nothing at all had happened and plopped down in front of her.

Wolfie bolted out from beneath the table with his head kept low and his ears lying flat against his head. Foxie's attention, however, remained fixed on Sofia and the leftover Chinese food. She waved her left paw, cocked her head to the side, then waved her right. This begging display would have been adorable if not for the fight that had preceded it.

"Stay," she told the Chow while she picked the pieces of chicken out from the container and dropped them onto a paper plate. Once she was certain there were no onions in the mix, she set the plate before Foxie and went to find Wolfie.

The larger dog sat waiting by her bedroom door, shaking fiercely and unwilling to make eye contact with her as she approached. As soon as she opened the door, he slipped into the dark room. She hated this, but at least Wolfie would be safe in there until she figured out a plan for Foxie.

Sofia definitely couldn't leave them together all day while she was at work tomorrow, but she couldn't exactly take Foxie back to the yard where she'd stolen her. She traced her way back to the kitchen where Foxie sat whining, the plate of food untouched.

"Umm, you can eat it now," she commanded.

Foxie shook and whined but didn't make a move for the food.

"Go ahead and eat."

Still nothing, so she used the edge of her foot to push the plate closer to Foxie. The dog still didn't budge.

"Okay, I—"

Foxie snapped to her feet and pushed her face into the food, consuming it so fast she had to gasp for air. *Weird.*

Sofia watched as the Chow inhaled every morsel

on the plate, licked it clean, and then began to eat the plate as well. As she wrestled the trash away, her phone dinged in her pocket with a Facebook notification. Sofia didn't keep many friends on social media. She mostly used it to share her designs and discuss techniques in her favorite frugal fashionista groups.

"Let go," she grunted, but Foxie had decided the battle for the plate was a fun game and clamped down harder.

"Foxie, no. Let go. Drop it."

On the last command, Foxie unclamped her jaw and let Sofia take control of the plate, which she promptly took to the trash.

Her phone dinged again.

"It's National Puppy Day!" Elizabeth Jane had posted, and already several comments had poured in.

"Here's Samson as a puppy and Samson now. Tagging all my dog-loving friends so they can share too!" The status was attached to a pair of photos showcasing Liz's giant dappled Akita—in her arms as a puppy and in her fiancé Dorian's arms now. She'd tagged at least forty people in her update, and Sofia was one of them.

Sofia would definitely not be sharing a photo of her ill-gotten dogs, but she *could* come to Elizabeth

Jane for help. After all, Liz had an entire ranch at her disposal. She could easily give Foxie a home or at least a safe place until Sofia figured out a better solution.

She called the Chow over and snapped a picture of her, then texted it to her friend.

Elizabeth Jane's reply came immediately: *Cute! Who's that?*

Sofia took a deep breath before typing: *Your new dog?*

*WHAT?!*

*I found her out wandering in the rain storm. She needs a home.*

*Why not with you?*

*Wolfie doesn't like her.*

*And you think Samson will?*

*I don't know, but she needs to go somewhere while I figure things out. Please will you take her in? Please! Please!*

Sofia watched as the three dots that meant her friend was typing appeared then disappeared then reappeared. If Liz refused to help, Sofia had no other options, other than maybe Blinky, D-Man, or one of their criminal friends. It seemed like a huge favor to ask people she'd only just met, though.

After a few moments pause, Sofia's phone rang.

"You owe me," Liz grumbled before hanging up.

# Sixteen

∽

Sofia shut Foxie into her bedroom before leaving for work the next day, giving Wolfie free reign of the larger apartment.

Although Elizabeth Jane had reluctantly agreed to take the Chow off Sofia's hands, she'd also said she would need a few days to prepare. And no matter how much Sofia begged, Liz refused to welcome Foxie in before Wednesday evening.

Today was only Monday.

It would be a long, long week.

Things weren't helped by the fact that Sofia's store was as empty as ever. Normally she liked having time alone with her thoughts, but today she would have welcomed a gaggle of screeching pre-teen shoppers if only for something to keep her busy.

The hours ticked by slowly until finally someone entered her shop. Not a customer, but rather Blinky coming by to gloat during his lunch break.

Sofia greeted him with a groan. "Don't look at me like that."

"Like what?" A snide grin spread across his rough features.

She drummed her fingers on the counter. "I don't know. The cat that ate the canary?"

Blinky laughed just like he always did. Could he really find everything in life this hilarious? "You, *my bird*," he said, "were a hit. Everyone loved you. Especially D-Man."

Sofia couldn't tell if what followed was a wink or a facial spasm, so she simply let out a sigh in response.

Blinky ignored her hesitation. Maybe he didn't really care. "Come out with us again this weekend. We'll be at the Ridge."

"Yeah, not really my scene." Sofia left the counter and paced to the nearest clothing rack, pretending to sort through the clothes and hoping Blinky would take the hint and leave her be.

"Oh, c'mon," he shouted, trailing after her. "Don't be so frigid."

She sighed again and moved on to the next rack. "That's really not how you talk to people when you want them to like you."

"Who said anything about liking me?" He crossed his arms over his chest and doubled over with laughter as he said, "You're D-Man's girl now."

"You know what, Blinky? I really think you should—"

Thankfully, a pair of shoppers entered her store before she could finish that sentence.

Sofia put on her sales voice and marched away from Blinky, his laughter trailing after her like a little lost puppy she just couldn't escape. "Can I help you find anything today, ladies?"

"You'll be there," he mumbled while walking past her to the exit and sidestepping the security detectors. "The Ridge. Saturday at eight. Don't forget, and don't make any excuses."

When Sofia finished helping the old women find new dresses for a friend's retirement party, she returned to the cash register to check her phone. A text from an unknown number awaited her: *Our date is tonight. Let me know when and where to pick you up.*

*D-Man?*

*What? Cheating on me already? This is Hunter.*

In all the excitement over Foxie, she'd somehow forgotten her deal with the charming cop. This was so not what she needed right now.

*I don't think I can make it. Sorry,* she typed then added a crying emoji.

*Nope, I already have everything planned, and I refuse to be stood up.*

This guy was never going to leave her alone. If she ignored him too long, he'd probably find her address in the police database and show up unannounced to take her on that date she'd stupidly agreed to. At least this way she'd know when he was coming and be able to keep him away from her apartment and the stolen dogs inside.

*Fine. 6:30,* she typed back after a quick moment to think it over. *Hoyt Street Apartments.*

*Don't sound too excited ;-)*

*Do I sound excited? Oops, that was a mistake.*

*Yeah, sure. Wear something you can move in. See you at 6:30!*

Sofia set her phone down and sighed. Normally she'd at least be a little excited about a mysterious date with a handsome semi-stranger. But everything in her life was so topsy-turvy these days, she honestly didn't know which way to look.

Just then, a middle-aged man came bustling into the store carrying a stack of papers. From the looks of his paint-splattered jeans and old concert T-shirt, he really didn't seem the type to waste money at Sofia's store, but something in his eyes told her he'd come for a different reason—and one she wouldn't like.

"Can I help you, sir?" she asked with that practiced friendly lilt that made her want to gag.

The man slammed a bright green paper onto the counter. "Can I put up this flyer?"

"We don't really..." Sofia glanced down and saw Foxie staring up at her in neon color. A lump of fear formed in her throat, cutting off the rest of what she'd wanted to say.

"*Please.*" The man regarded her with equal parts agitation and desperation. "That's my Fanta. The kids named her after the soda. Cute, right? She went missing last night in the storm, and we think someone might have taken her. There's a reward."

He pointed to the bottom of the flyer where the words $100 REWARD were written in capital letters and underlined three times. "It's not a lot, but it's all we can offer. Name's Joe Collins. My number's here." He jabbed his finger back at the flyer, but Sofia kept her eyes glued to his face instead. "Will you keep an eye out for her? Call me if you see anything?"

Sofia gulped then put on the biggest fake smile of her entire life. "Yes, of course, I will. Good luck."

But the man hadn't stuck around for longer than it took to catch her nod of agreement. He'd already begun his retreat, leaving Sofia alone with her shame.

# Seventeen

S ofia thought about her Foxie-Fanta conundrum the rest of that afternoon. If the man with the flyers and his family truly loved their dog so much, then why had they left her out in the pouring rain?

Had she somehow misread the situation? And if so, what could she actually do about this problem? It's not like she could drive back over and return the dog to its yard.

By the end of her shift, she decided to go ahead with her plan to deliver Foxie to Elizabeth Jane's ranch Wednesday evening. If Liz saw the flyers, *she* could return the dog. Otherwise...well, it served the guy right for being so negligent.

Pinpricks of both sadness and relief pierced her heart when she realized no one had come looking for Wolfie, and he'd been with Sofia for nearly a week. Even though she hadn't figured out the right call when it came to Foxie—or rather *Fanta*—Sofia felt certain she had saved Wolfie's life with her willingness to act on his behalf.

Yes, she stood firmly on the moral high ground here...

So then why did she still feel guilty?

Maybe it just came with the territory. Or maybe she'd eventually stop feeling the stinging residue of shame.

*Maybe, maybe.*

She arrived home at 6:12, which left barely enough time to get the dogs outside for a bathroom break, let alone any time to change her outfit and refresh her makeup for this date with Hunter. So she'd skip the getting ready part, big deal. The absolute last thing she needed was to be caught red-handed by her new cop boyfriend.

Luckily, this wasn't a date. Not really. It was more of a compromise.

They'd go on their one date, and Sofia would make certain he would not ask for another. Tonight's outing simply needed to happen so that he would lose interest and move on. Honestly, she was surprised he hadn't already.

"Hurry, hurry," she urged Fanta as the Chow walked the perimeter of the courtyard, sniffing everything but peeing on nothing. After five minutes of their jaunty little stroll, she gave up and returned Fanta to the apartment. Wolfie peed everywhere already, so it wouldn't really be that big of a deal if Fanta had an accident inside, too.

"Mmm, I love a woman who isn't afraid to get down and dirty." Hunter came right up behind her just as she was reaching down to pick up Wolfie's doggie doo in a tiny plastic baggie.

Sofia popped up so fast her head spun from the motion. "You shouldn't sneak up on people like that!" She glowered at Hunter as she did her best to tie the bag angrily and without losing a shred of her hard-won dignity.

Wolfie yipped and tugged on the leash in his desperation to greet their visitor.

Hunter laughed as Wolfie licked every inch of his outstretched hand. "You have nothing to be embarrassed about. Gotta take care of your dogs, right?"

"Dogs?" Sofia frowned. What did Hunter know?

Was this date some kind of ruse? Was he already on to her dognapping ways? "I only have one."

"And *I* also have one, which makes two."

Sofia knew the Anchorage PD had better things to do than scope out a two-time dognapper, but still she couldn't help feeling as if she were being sized up.

Guilty conscience? Maybe. Flustered nerves? Definitely.

"Yeah, yeah, whatever," Sofia said with a quick roll of her eyes. "You wait here. I'll be right back."

Hunter followed her down the sidewalk. "Can I come with you? See where you live?"

"I'd rather not," she said, hoping that answer would be enough. She already had a hard time keeping track of her various lies regarding the dogs and really didn't want to add any more. "Besides, it will just be a second. I have to put him back and wash my hands. I'll be right down."

"Okay, then. I'll be waiting over there." Hunter shrugged and pointed toward a patrol car that sat idling by the curb. Sofia hadn't noticed it before now, but the sudden thought of driving around in the police cruiser sent bile surging up from her stomach. It burned when she swallowed it back down, but at least she knew this particular date wouldn't be ending with a kiss at the doorstep.

Hunter reached for her arm to help steady her. "Whoa, are you okay?"

Sofia nodded and resisted his attempts to support her the rest of the way to the door.

*Get a hold of yourself, Stepanov!*

Back inside, she swished a bit of mouthwash then grabbed her purse and turned back toward the door.

Wolfie rubbed his head against her hip and whined.

She made the mistake of looking into his amber eyes, and her heart cracked in two. "I'm sorry, buddy. I'll be back as soon as I can. Then the day after tomorrow we get to visit a ranch. Won't that be fun?"

Even the dog could tell her forced cheer wasn't sincere. He groaned before skulking away and tucking himself underneath the table.

Sofia wished she had the option to join him there. They could all hide until Hunter eventually gave up and drove off in his stupid cruiser.

"I'll be back soon," she promised Wolfie one last time, then padded out into the hall and locked the door behind her.

Even though she'd only known Hunter for a

grand total of seventeen minutes, she knew their evening together would be a memorable one.

All she had to do was stay cool and do her best to resist his charms...

How hard could that be?

# Eighteen

ᔕ~ᔐ

lthough Sofia didn't immediately spot Hunter waiting for her when she stepped out of the building, a *blip-blip* from the cruiser at the curb drew her eye to the idling vehicle, the passenger door open and waiting.

"Sure you don't want me in the back?" she joked and immediately regretted when Hunter gave his answer...

"Oh, I want you in the back, but that's not really a first date kind of thing."

Sofia turned away before he could even finish his horrible comeback. She could feel his eyes on her but refused to look his way, instead choosing to cross her arms over her chest and stare pointedly out the side window.

"Relax. I'm only kidding," he assured her with a soft voice. "You can't set me up like that and then expect me not to make a joke."

She sighed and risked a glance his way. At least his silly, flirtatious overture was better than having to admit she was, in fact, fit for the criminal cage in back.

Hunter held one hand on the steering wheel and the other over his heart. "My apologies, Miss Sofia. I promise to be a perfect gentleman for the rest of the night."

He looked so corny as he awaited her response that Sofia couldn't help but laugh and relax into her seat. "Thank you," she said with a sincere smile, mostly because she was happy to be moving away from this topic. "Now, what are these big plans of yours?"

Hunter shifted into drive and pulled away from the curb. "Tonight I'm going to show you the unseen side of Anchorage."

"I've lived here my whole life. There is no unseen side as far as I'm concerned."

"That's where you're wrong. Certain areas open up to you only when you know the right people... or when you have a badge." He flashed a smile her way before merging into traffic and heading south.

She laughed at the serious look on his face. Hunter Burke was hot stuff and boy, did he know it. "So we'll be abusing your police privileges tonight," she said with a smirk. "Got it."

"Hey, I risk my life on a daily basis for this city. I deserve some perks, don't I?"

Sofia shrugged. "If you say so. So, tell me about these unseen areas."

"I don't need to... Because we're already here." Hunter put the car into park right in front of an old, abandoned warehouse Sofia had passed by every single day on her way to work.

"Unseen?" She laughed and shook her head. "I literally see this building every day."

Hunter's eyes lit with the promise of adventure. "Yeah, but have you seen the inside?"

She studied the expansive gray building before her. The windows had been boarded up with giant wood slabs, and a fresh swatch of graffiti adorned its street-facing facade. It did not look like somewhere Sofia wanted to be—especially not on a date.

"Umm, isn't it a homeless camp?" she asked.

"Nah, that's just a rumor. We cleared those guys out years ago. C'mon." Hunter climbed out of the car, and Sofia followed suit. "Are you ready?" he asked, reaching his hand toward hers.

"I'll try to contain my excitement," she mumbled, allowing him to clutch her hand as they walked toward a hidden entrance around back.

Hunter reached into his pocket and pulled out a small flashlight, then unbolted the door and pushed it open. Particles of dust danced in the beam from the new light source. Even though the evening sky was still light above, the inside of the warehouse was practically pitch black.

"They boarded everything up to keep people out," Hunter explained, tugging her through the door. "Luckily, I have a key."

Sofia gulped down the knot of fear in her throat, thankful now that Hunter had already decided to hold her hand. She had never been a fan of the dark. Even though the blackness was meant to hide things, it seemed to her that the night had a way of bringing hidden things out into the open.

Scary things and people. Secrets that would be better left untold.

"It's okay," Hunter said, sensing her nerves, which couldn't have been too difficult given the gooseflesh that had formed on her arms and the shiver that overtook her entire body. "I've got you," he said as he gave her hand a reassuring squeeze. "Nothing bad is going to happen."

"Another promise?" She attempted a laugh, but it took too much energy to pull off properly. "That makes two now."

Hunter's voice came out strong and sure, as if he wasn't afraid of anything in the entire world. "And here comes one more. I promise you'll like this place once I show you what's inside."

Sofia doubted that very much, but allowed Hunter to pull her deeper into the abandoned warehouse, nonetheless.

After about twenty paces, Hunter stopped. "Take out your phone," he instructed.

She did as he said and switched on the flashlight app. While her attention was focused elsewhere, Hunter pushed his tactical light into Sofia's palm then stepped behind her and put one hand on her waist. The other gently took hold of her wrist.

"The phone is for taking a video," he explained.

She didn't need a video. Honestly, the only thing she needed was to leave this place as soon as possible. "Of what?"

"That's what I'd like to show you," he mumbled, his face hovering a few inches above her shoulder, so close she could feel the warmth of his breath caress her cheek.

He used his hand to guide hers, and together

they illuminated an old piece of machinery that must have been at least fifteen feet wide. They revealed the gears, cylinders, and metal a few inches at a time, tracing over it several times before Sofia could appreciate the full picture.

"It's a textile machine," Hunter said just as Sofia had figured it out for herself. "This used to be a clothing factory. At the vet, when you told me you design clothes, I immediately thought of this place. It used to provide a lot of jobs to people who needed them around here. Maybe one day you can open it again to sell *Fashions by Sofia*."

"*Vigilante*," she whispered. "My line is called *Vigilante*."

"Hmm, I like it," he said, squeezing her hand again before letting go of her wrist. He let his other hand linger on her waist as she continued to study the machine.

"I know the dark makes you uncomfortable, so we don't need to stay. I just wanted you to see this place, to know that sometimes things aren't what they appear to be from the outside, that sometimes a very different kind of treasure is waiting for those who are willing to tread into the dark."

Sofia turned into him, forgetting how close he already stood. Her shiver returned, but this one was of anticipation rather than dread. "That's a very strange thing to say."

"Yeah, well, I'm a bit of a strange guy." Hunter wrapped both arms around her waist and held her close for a few moments before letting go and once again offering her his hand. "Okay, so that was part one of the night I have planned for us. Ready for part two?"

Oh, was she ever...

# Nineteen

"I can't believe you remembered," Sofia said as she and Hunter settled back into the off-duty cruiser.

"What? That you like clothes?" He shrugged before jamming the key in the ignition and bringing the car back to life. "You told me the first time we met, and I could tell from the way you said it that it was important to you. Why wouldn't I want to remember?"

None of Sofia's boyfriends—not that there had been many—ever showed an interest in her flare for fashion. The fact that Hunter, who hardly knew her, was already supporting her interests and encouraging her dreams meant more than she wanted to admit. "You actually like me, don't you?" she whispered.

He waited for her to look at him before saying, "I actually do. What on earth would have told you otherwise?"

"I... I don't know," she mumbled.

Hunter reached for her hand again and held it tight. "Now the question is whether you could actually like me, too."

If Sofia swore not to commit any more crimes, would that make dating Hunter okay? Because, oh, did she want it to be. She swallowed her hesitation, finally willing to allow herself the chance to find happiness with Hunter. "I think—"

Static broke through the speakers, interrupting Sofia midsentence. "Burke. You there?" the dispatcher said.

Hunter let go of her hand, breaking the magic that flowed between them. He groaned, but pushed the button to speak anyway. "Kind of busy now."

"Your buddy Collins is back at the station. Ranting and raving, telling anyone who will listen that some hardened criminal stole his dog."

Hunter did not sound happy. Didn't look it, either. "Did you tell him we're keeping an eye out?" he barked to the dispatcher.

*Joe Collins.*

*The stolen dog she called Foxie.*

Sofia's crimes had caught up with her yet again. They'd come to haunt her at the very moment she'd given herself permission to enjoy her date. There could be no future with Hunter, because there would always be the guilt. This realization gripped Sofia in the guts and twisted hard.

"I did, but he demanded to speak to you personally." The dispatcher's words were hardly audible over the pounding in Sofia's head.

"Well, too bad," Hunter snapped, his anger startling her. "I'm off duty—and on a date."

The dispatcher chuckled, then said, "Hi, girl who's crazy enough to go out with Burke."

"Umm, hi," Sofia mumbled, her cheeks burning as she did.

"Tell Collins I'll call him in the morning."

Another laugh. "He's not going to like that."

"Too bad," Hunter snapped again, shooting an apologetic expression Sofia's way. "I have more important things on my mind than a runaway dog and its crazy owner. I'll call him tomorrow, or not at all. Let him pick."

"On it." The radio clicked back to silence, and Hunter sighed as he offered Sofia a tense smile. "Sorry about that. You were saying?" He reached for her hand, but she yanked it away as if she'd been stung.

She needed to end this—end it now before Hunter charmed her any further. She clenched both hands to her stomach and cast her eyes toward her feet. "I was about to say that I think I'm really sick after all. Would you mind taking me home?"

He studied her for a moment, almost as if he didn't believe her, almost as if he somehow knew that Collins's dognapper sat right here beside him. "Are you sure? I was going to take you to the top of Conoco-Phillips for dinner and maybe a little dancing in the starlight, if weather permits."

Sofia frowned. He really had planned a special night for her, but the gnawing guilt in her gut would never let up enough for her to truly enjoy his company. Hunter deserved better than some low-life criminal who'd lied to his face every second since meeting him.

He deserved so much more than Sofia.

Hunter twisted the key in the ignition, bringing the car to silence. "Is it the call? I'm sorry work followed me out tonight. This guy's dog ran away and he insists somebody stole it, said he saw a red sedan pull up in the rain, but I say he's full of it. Let's forget it and enjoy the rest of our night, shall we?"

Sofia wanted to agree. She wanted to see where things could go with Hunter, a man who liked her enough to pay attention to her interests, to plan something special just for her. Under any other circumstances, she'd be thrilled to find herself on the arm of such a handsome, thoughtful, funny man— but not tonight, not like this.

She needed to tell him no. Her sanity depended on it.

Yes, she wished she could tell him everything, let him know it wasn't his fault, that she actually liked him a whole heck of a lot, but...

Before she could say anything at all, her stomach roiled in protest at all the mixed emotions churning through her core. It was only by some miracle of mercy she managed to open the door fast enough to throw up the contents of her stomach onto the pavement outside.

# Twenty

Sofia's Monday ended with her curled around the toilet bowl. But no matter how much she emptied from her stomach, the guilt remained. Wolfie stood guard in the hallway, whining occasionally as he waited for Sofia to come to bed.

Meanwhile, Foxie contented herself with a Kong toy Blinky had stolen for them as part of that first batch of doggie supplies. *How long ago that seemed!*

Tuesday started out much the same, but Sofia's checking account couldn't afford anymore sick time. She also couldn't afford the wrath of the franchise owner, should she request yet another day off so close to the string of days she'd taken last week.

So she sucked it up, dragged herself from bed, skipped the makeup, and pulled herself to work for yet another slow, boring day. A part of her feared Joe Collins would return with another stack of flyers, but luckily he didn't make a second appearance that day. If he had, Sofia might have sobbingly confessed the whole thing, weakened as she was now from the physical manifestation of her anxiety.

She wondered if Collins was with Hunter at the station now, describing the very make and model of Sofia's car, putting her former date on the trail to her arrest. Could she be taken into custody for dognapping? And if so, would Hunter show her mercy?

As if the very thought had summoned him, a text from Hunter lit up Sofia's phone: *Are you feeling better today?*

*Yeah, I'm doing okay. Sorry about last night.*

*Me too. I ended up eating both our dinners. Could barely button my pants this morning.*

*LOL.* She smiled despite her newfound resolve to avoid Hunter. If only things could have been different. She set her phone aside just as it buzzed with a new text.

*So...* Hunter had written.

She waited for him to type more, holding back the urge to fill the blank screen with her confession.

*Now that you're doing better, can we try again?*

Doing better? Yeah right. The moment she saw Hunter, it would all come spilling out yet again. There was no better, only further—further away from Hunter's searching gaze, further from the guilt over taking Foxie, further from all of it. Seeing Hunter again would send her sliding back into that sticky swamp of guilt.

She just couldn't.

*I'm sorry, Hunter. I don't think that's such a good idea.*

His answer came back immediately. *But why?*

*I just...* She erased the last two words and thought. What could she possibly say that would be enough to deter him?

Before she could type anything else, another text appeared from Hunter: *I know you like me. I could feel it when we were in the factory.*

She sighed. Why did he have to be a cop? If he were anyone else, she could share her guilt and move on... But with him? Impossible.

*Maybe, but I'm not really looking for a relationship right now,* she answered at last.

*Then let's take a relationship off the table. Can't we at least be friends?*

There was nothing left to say, nothing she could

say without telling him everything. Perhaps if she stopped responding he'd take the hint.

Just as she was about to officially give up on their conversation, another message filled her screen, this time from a number she didn't recognize.

*Hey. This is Matt! Got your number from Blinky... Anyway, it was really great meeting you this weekend, and I heard you were invited to come to the Ridge with us. This is me seconding that invite. I know we aren't into each other like that, but I'd still really like to have you around as a friend. Man, this is getting rambly. Anyway, please say you'll come. By the way, this is Matt.*

And a second later: *Oh, I already said that it was me. Darn it. Okay, I'll go die of embarrassment now. Bye.*

Sofia laughed, thankful for the texts from D-Man to distract her from the argument with Hunter.

*Don't die,* she typed while chuckling to herself. *As long as you're going, I'll be there, too.*

At least she wouldn't have to die alone. She had Wolfie and new friends that suited her recent, otherwise questionable activities. One day, when the time was right, there would be other boyfriends. Other men.

But would any of them make Sofia's heart flitter the way Hunter did?

# Twenty-One

F inally, Wednesday arrived. Hopefully once she'd handed Foxie over to Elizabeth Jane, Sofia's guilt would be at least partially abated. Together, she and Wolfie could make a new normal. They could spend time simply enjoying each other's company—as a dog and his person were meant to do.

Despite all the drama surrounding Foxie, Sofia and Wolfie were becoming closer by the day. The large wolf hybrid had now taken to sleeping beside Sofia's bed rather than his previous place under the dining room table. So, whenever she startled awake from a nightmare, she could calm herself in an instant by dropping her arm over the edge of the mattress and stroking Wolfie's thick, downy fur.

Sofia's friend Liz had always referred to her Akita, Samson, as her baby, but Sofia had come to think of Wolfie more like a partner than as her child. His constant presence reassured her that she had done a good thing by saving him.

Whatever happened with Foxie, Joe Collins, or even Hunter, Sofia was secure in the knowledge that she had done at least one thing right. *Important.*

And knowing this kept her going, even on the most difficult of days.

Especially as she passed the abandoned textile factory on her way to work each morning, remembered her time with Hunter—and the fact that it could never happen again.

He'd texted her several times since their date had come to an abrupt end the previous evening. Eventually she'd had to turn her phone off to avoid giving in to her intense urge to respond. She'd tried to lose herself in a reality TV marathon, but the show's petty drama only heightened her anxiety.

*If only* she had such minor concerns as finding out who stole Jenny's weave or hatching a plan to receive a charming bachelor's rose. What had once been a guilty pleasure held no entertainment for her now.

Worse still, her hands trembled too much for her

to work at the sewing machine. Ultimately, she ended up going to bed more than two hours early with the hope that she'd feel better after a proper night's rest.

Instead, she woke up feeling as if her head were stuffed with cotton and her stomach filled with scorpions. These sensations further intensified when Preeti turned up in her store shortly after opening.

"Good morning," Preeti said brightly, making Sofia feel guilty for wishing the other girl would simply disappear.

"Hi," Sofia said, accepting an overly familiar hug from this acquaintance she hardly knew.

"Blinky said you could hook me up," Preeti whispered in Sofia's ear before pulling away and continuing the conversation at full volume. "I need a few new outfits for work and dates and stuff. You know," she finished, tossing a subtle wink Sofia's way.

*Wait...*

*Is Preeti actually asking me to steal from my work?*

This question was answered but a second later when Preeti dropped a pair of silk underwear into the large shoulder bag at her side.

Sofia cleared her throat and put herself between Preeti and the security camera that hung nearby in the rear corner of the store. She did *not* need this today. "What are you doing?" she whisper-yelled.

"Shopping," Preeti said with an exaggerated roll of her eyes. "Like I told you, Blinky said you could help me find what I'm looking for. You know, like he helped you with the supplies for your new dog. Where'd you get him again?"

Wow, this girl was clearly not Sofia's friend—and she was beginning to doubt that Blinky ever had been either.

Still...

What could Sofia do besides look the other way and refuse to get involved?

If she turned Preeti away, then Wolfie would be at risk yet again. This all would have been for nothing. She couldn't let that happen. Couldn't let Wolfie down when she'd promised to keep him safe.

But she *could* stop fraternizing with Blinky and his gang of merry thieves. Maybe he'd been right about her. Maybe she was only a rebel in appearance after all.

And, you know what? That was just fine with her.

# Twenty-Two

After work, Sofia packed up both dogs and drove the twenty miles to Liz's ranch on the southern outskirts of town. She kept Wolfie in the backseat and let Foxie sit shotgun in hopes of avoiding any mid-journey dog fights.

And although Sofia and Elizabeth Jane had kept in touch, this would be Sofia's first time visiting Memory Ranch. She found herself astonished by the enormous size of her former coworker's ranch estate. Sofia's entire neighborhood could fit inside the mostly empty piece of land. Just when she thought she'd reached the end of the drive, more would unfold before her. After what felt like miles and miles of fields, she passed a pole barn followed by a horse stable, and finally discovered the old farm house tucked into the very back of the property, the backdrop of foggy mountains stretching proudly across the horizon.

Sofia put her little red car in park, then opened the passenger door to let the first dog out. Foxie immediately sprinted toward the wrap-around porch where Liz and her fiancé Dorian waited with outstretched arms.

"Wow, what a pretty girl you are!" Liz cried, bending down to hug the big, fluffy Chow.

Liz's Akita whined on the other side of the screen door and rattled it with his huge paws.

"You'll get your turn, Samson. Just let us say hi first," Dorian called to the whimpering sled dog in a high-pitched baby voice as he stroked Foxie's soft mane.

Satisfied that Foxie was behaving herself, Sofia grabbed a leash from her glovebox and hooked Wolfie in. Gently she coaxed him from the car, which took more work than expected. The big dog stayed glued to her side, unsure of the new place and new people and still very much unsure about Foxie.

"Hi again, Wolfie," Liz called, jogging over to offer Sofia a quick hug and Wolfie a scratch between his ears.

"This place is insane," Sofia said, spotting a tiny speck on the rear horizon she assumed was the pole barn she'd passed on their way in.

Liz laughed and gave her visitor another hug. "We still have a lot of work to do, but it's really coming along. By the way, this is Dorian." She turned and gestured back toward the porch, but Dorian was too busy playing with Foxie to hear his name being called.

"We've met," Sofia reminded Elizabeth Jane, but failed to mention the dark circumstances of their first meeting. Liz and Dorian had obviously moved on from that, which meant Sofia should, too. "Hi, Dorian!" she called with a friendly wave.

Dorian strode over with a panting Foxie at his side, a huge smile stretched across his face. "So, tell me again how you found this big girl."

Sofia had prepared for this question and rehearsed exactly what she would say. Hopefully this would be the last lie she'd need to tell regarding either of her ill-gotten dogs.

She shrugged to lighten the mood, just in case any anxiety reverberated in her words. "She was just walking on her own in the pouring rain last weekend. I opened my car door to check it out, and she hopped right in on top of me."

Liz and Dorian both laughed. Thankfully, they believed her recounting of events to be real. Maybe one day Sofia would be able to believe this modified version of the truth, too.

"Didn't you find this guy on the side of the road, too?" Dorian asked, giving Wolfie a firm scratch on the ribs.

Sofia's breath hitched. Dorian had once been a private investigator and was now a student at the local police academy. Maybe *Hunter* couldn't see past his romantic interest in Sofia, but Dorian's judgment wouldn't be similarly clouded. She needed to be much more careful here.

"Yeah," she said with a fake laugh. "I guess I need to start driving some new roads. No more room in my apartment, what with this huge thing taking up all the space."

Dorian nodded and returned his attention to Foxie.

"I'm going to bring out Samson to say hello," Elizabeth Jane announced, turning on her heel. Foxie trotted after her, so the others followed, too.

"Samson," Liz said, opening the door slowly. "Meet your new sister, Foxie. Actually..." She closed the door again, frustrating the dogs on both sides of the screen. She frowned and asked, "Sofia, would you be too offended if I renamed her? Not that *Foxie* isn't great, but how perfect would it be if we called her *Delilah*?"

"Pretty perfect," Sofia agreed.

Liz sighed her relief, then swung the screen door wide open.

All three massive dogs jumped into a vigorous sniffing session, red, gray, and black fur mixed to form a giant ball of waggly fluff. Round and round they went, until at last Samson dropped to his front paws, wagging his curved tail high in the air behind him. Foxie responded in kind, and soon the two new canine siblings were chasing each other down the dirt driveway and out toward the far reaches of the property.

Wolfie, on the other hand, stuck close to Sofia's side despite no longer being clipped into his leash. He preferred to watch the action rather than be a part of it. Sofia couldn't blame him, either.

"Best friends already!" Dorian cried, looping an arm around Liz's waist as the two watched the happy dogs with a pair of equally satisfied smiles.

She closed her eyes and silently prayed that Joe Collins would drop his search and let Fanta-Foxie-

Delilah live out her days here at the ranch with the new family that already loved her very much.

Otherwise, Sofia would never be able to forgive herself.

# Twenty-Three

S ofia sat on the porch with Elizabeth Jane while Dorian worked on preparing dinner for everyone inside.

"I never would have guessed you'd end up here," Sofia said as she watched Foxie and Samson lumber across the open field. Tongues hung out the side of each dog's mouth, but still they ran and played despite their obvious fatigue. Wolfie remained uninterested in their antics as he snored peacefully at the base of her rocking chair.

"Where? With a man that cooks?" Liz asked, closing her eyes as she leaned her head back with a smile. "Yeah, that surprised me, too."

"That, but all the rest of it, too. The ranch, going back to college, getting married. *All of it.*" Sofia realized for the first time that she was jealous of all her friend had. Maybe that was why she hadn't made much—or really, *any*—time to visit her lately.

Liz leaned forward, placing an elbow on each knee and propping her chin in her hands. "I'm not lucky like you, Sofia. I never knew who I wanted to be until..."

"I know. You don't have to explain." The past year had been hard on Elizabeth Jane, and the last thing Sofia wanted to do was force her to relive all the horrible, ugly memories that had delivered her to this seemingly perfect place.

Her guilt returned, this time with a new flavor. How could she envy her friend's happiness? Sofia's troubles were caused by no one but herself, but Liz had been to hell and back at no fault of her own.

Sofia placed a hand on her friend's shoulder. "And just so you know, I struggle with that, too."

Liz looked up at her, a confused expression splashed across her freckled face. "With knowing who you are?"

Sofia nodded and prayed Liz wouldn't ask for an explanation. She felt so close to cracking open and letting all her secrets escape into the world.

"No way am I buying that. You're the strongest person I've ever met. Nothing gets under your skin.

It's like you never have to question who you are or what you want."

Sofia swallowed back the angry laugh that bubbled in her gut. If Liz's statements had once been true... well, they weren't any longer. Sofia hardly recognized the woman she saw in the mirror these days. The passion she had once felt for life had gotten lost beneath the thick and overwhelming fog of guilt.

If Liz couldn't see that yet, she would one day—and likely soon. Especially if the worst happened with her new Chow.

"Thanks for saying that," she murmured. She had once been that strong person her friend admired. Perhaps she could find a way to be that person again.

"What have you been up to lately?" Liz asked, having no idea how her words pricked at Sofia's already fatigued conscience.

She shrugged. "Oh, you know... Work, dog, life."

Liz laughed. "Sounds about right."

"Dinner's almost ready!" Dorian called from inside.

A goofy smile lit up Elizabeth Jane's face. "Have I mentioned how much I love that man?"

"At least a dozen odd times," Sofia answered with a smile. Her friend deserved a partner who doted on her the way Dorian did. Sofia had once thought she deserved such a man herself, but now she knew better.

"How about you?" Liz asked as she rocked idly in her chair. "Seeing anyone special?"

Sofia shook her head sadly. In another life, one in which she'd made different decisions, she'd be gushing hearts and flowers as she told her friend every last detail about the dreamy Hunter Burke. In this life, however, she kept her mouth firmly shut. Hunter wasn't hers to discuss, nor would he ever be.

Liz's eyes flashed with the spark of an idea. "You know, Dorian has made a lot of hot friends at the academy. I bet—"

"What was that, my darling Liz?" Dorian asked, appearing on the porch wearing an apron and waving a spatula.

"I was just saying that maybe we could set Sofia up with one of your hot cop friends."

"I didn't realize you found my friends so attractive," he said with a good-natured chuckle. "I guess that means it's time for me to make some new, uglier ones."

"Calm down," Liz cooed as she crossed the porch and tucked herself into her fiancé's arms. "You know you're the only man for me. I was just doing some... uh, *window shopping* for my single friend."

Dorian rolled his eyes and made a goofy face. "Wow, I feel objectified on behalf of my gender."

"Oh, whatever. You like it," Elizabeth Jane teased.

"Not sure *I like it*, but I'm one-hundred percent certain *I love you.*"

Sofia looked away as the engaged couple shared a long, lingering kiss.

Finally placing her jealousy aside, she truly felt happy for her friend. Unfortunately, the more time she spent with this lovey-dovey pair, the more she felt as if she'd been robbed at her chance to one day find the same happiness.

It was funny how one little decision could snowball into other bigger decisions, which could then change everything so fast that you no longer even knew who you were.

Sofia hoped that one day she would figure that out again.

But until then...

She'd have to take it one day at a time. Starting with finding a way to get through tonight.

# Twenty-Four

Sofia didn't know what she had done to deserve Dorian's homemade chicken and biscuits. The creamy, buttery goodness tasted amazing going in, but quickly sunk like a rock in her bile-ridden stomach. This meal had become a unique blend of both ecstasy and torture, and apparently her hosts noticed.

"Don't you like it?" Liz whispered when Dorian returned to the stove to fetch second helpings for himself and Liz.

Sofia puffed out her cheeks and put a hand on her stomach. "It's delicious, but I'm trying to watch my weight."

"What? Why? You're perfect." Liz stared blankly

at Sofia as if this declaration was somehow impossible to believe.

She laughed at her friend's befuddled expression. "If only I could just date you, half of my problems would be solved right there."

Elizabeth Jane made a kissy face and batted her eyelashes, sending both women into a fit of giggles. It felt so good to laugh for a change.

"Hey, no moving in on my woman!" Dorian joked, setting a steaming plate of comfort food before his fiancée, then taking his seat at the head of the table.

As her two companions dug in to their generous second helpings, Sofia's phone vibrated beside her half-empty plate. Expecting it to be Hunter, she was surprised when she saw that the text had instead come from D-Man: *SOS!!!*

"Everything okay?" Liz asked. Her eyebrows pinched as she glanced from Sofia's phone back to her face.

"Umm, yeah, but I just need to take this. Be right back." Sofia pushed her chair back and raced out the door just as her ringtone began to chime.

"What's going on?" she said after pushing the accept call button.

D-Man's breath came out in jagged bursts,

making it hard for Sofia to understand the words between. "I'm... There was... I just came back from a deal, and—"

"Wait." She climbed into her car and shut the door. It was the best she could do for privacy under these circumstances. "Matt, hang on. A deal?"

He groaned impatiently. "You know, the reason they call me D-Man."

*Of course.* She felt like an idiot for not immediately understanding.

"Anyway..." He took another extended breath. "I saw this group of guys ducking into that old building on Eureka that has been abandoned forever, so I followed them."

Sofia pinched the bridge of her nose. She could already tell this conversation was headed in a direction she would not like. "What? Why would you follow them?"

"I wanted to see what was going on. Thought I might be able to find some new clientele."

She groaned at his stupidity, at knowing that whatever came next would undoubtedly be worse still. "Go on."

"There were a bunch of cages lined against a wall. Dogs jammed into them so tight most of them couldn't stand. And—" His voice broke. It took him a moment to compose himself again.

Sofia waited. There was nothing she could say until Matt told her his full story.

At last, he continued. "A guy at the door was collecting money. He asked me to place a bet. I still didn't know what was going on, so I said, 'against the odds.' He laughed and took my money, then pushed me toward the small crowd gathered around the center of the room. They brought out two of the dogs, and..."

Sofia was startled when D-Man began to cry. She wished she could offer him a hug or provide some greater comfort than simply just listening on the other end of a cell wave.

"I-I-I watched as this huge sled dog ripped off the muzzle of a smaller mutt. He just—He just tore off part of its face. Blood was everywhere, and I—"

"Matt, stop. I don't want to hear anymore." Sofia hated that an illegal dog ring was operating so close to her own home, hated that D-Man had stumbled upon such a gruesome scene, and hated that there was nothing she could do to help.

D-Man wept openly, still gasping for breath. "I can't stop picturing it. It was the most awful thing I've ever seen."

"I know. I'm so sorry." Sofia couldn't stop picturing it, either. She imagined Wolfie in the ring, scared for his life, and had to hold back tears of her own. Matt needed her to be strong now. *That is why he called... Right?*

"C-can you help me?" *Well, apparently not.*

"Help? With what?" A weight formed in her stomach, pulling her down deeper into the seat. If only she could sink, sink so far into the depths that no one knew where to find her. That things like this would stop happening, stop pulling her in.

Matt's voice held hope. "Blinky told me you saved a dog that was being abused."

"I don't actually know what Wolfie's story was. I don't think I—"

"There were so many dogs, and there will be more. We could—"

"I'm not an expert or anything." She rushed to cut off every single argument he made. She could not get involved. They could not mount such a dangerous rescue. How could she make D-Man understand?

"I've only taken a couple dogs from people's yards," she tried. "Never anything like this."

After a pause, Matt spoke again, his voice now steady, sure of its path. "We have to rescue them,

Sofia. I didn't know who else to call, and I'm going to find a way to help the dogs with or without you. But I'd rather it be with you. Please say you'll help."

Sofia felt the grip on her heart tighten, tighten, squeeze. These dogs needed her. Her friend needed her. If she refused to help, the dogs would die. Matt would have a difficult time rescuing them on his own. If he was caught, would the ringleaders punish him? Would the cops pick him up, find out about his drug-dealing business, and lock him away forever—all because he wanted to do something good?

There wasn't a choice here. Not for Sofia.

"Okay," she said at last. "When?"

# Twenty-Five

S ofia left the ranch shortly after her call with
D-Man. Not too long ago, she'd vowed to
extricate herself from Blinky's group and
stop committing crimes, allowing herself and Wolfie
to finally move on with their lives.

But how could she refuse to help the poor dogs
D-Man had discovered? They had it even worse than
Wolfie did, and if they weren't rescued, they would
all die horrible, violent deaths.

And it would be entirely her fault.

So, *of course* she'd agreed not only to help, but to
orchestrate the rescue herself. It would happen on
Saturday night. She'd come along to the Ridge as
invited, but she and Matt would leave early together.

This would provide them with the alibi they needed in case things went sour.

D-Man would secure the supplies—crates, food, a pair of cargo vans. Sofia's only condition was that he not tell her how he obtained them. She'd already willfully broken enough laws to last a lifetime.

Another task that fell to Sofia was to find a place they could take the dogs once rescued. And, thanks to Hunter, she already knew exactly where to go— the old textile factory. D-Man said he could easily shimmy the lock, and Sofia would sneak in the supplies before heading to the Ridge on Saturday night.

It all made perfect sense.

The only thing they hadn't planned was the long-term effects of the rescue and where the dogs would eventually end up after she and Matt removed them from the fighting ring. Many would presumably be too far gone to find new homes, but Sofia vowed to try and save them all.

Maybe if she gave herself a couple weeks, she could train and rehabilitate them enough that someone would be willing to give each of them a second chance at forever. She hoped this would be the case, but if nothing else, the poor abused dogs could at least find merciful, comfortable deaths in the arms of a caring veterinarian rather than being torn to shreds for the amusement of the very worst kind of human beings.

Considering either of these possibilities brought tears to her eyes. She hated that she might not be able to save them all, but if even one dog moved on to a better life, then this would all be worth it.

Wolfie nuzzled her palm and smiled at her. She loved his doggie grins, especially since he always seemed to know exactly when Sofia needed one. Midnight had arrived, and though Sofia doubted she'd catch any sleep, she invited Wolfie into the bed and cuddled him through the night.

The next morning, Sofia went to work, praying there would be no more surprises—no more shoplifting, dogfighting, lying to friends—*nothing*. Miraculously, she made it through the entire work day without any added drama, which was good since she could barely grapple with the heavy anxiety that weighed her down already.

Just as she planned to declare this day a good one, another friend decided to call in a favor. This time, it was Elizabeth Jane.

Sofia took a deep breath before answering. *Please just let this be a happy, catch-up call and not the start of a new crisis.* "Hey, Liz. How's Foxie... I mean *Delilah* doing?"

Liz's voice came out quiet despite the excitement of her words. "Oh my gosh, she is just wonderful. Samson and I love her so much already, but that's not why I'm calling."

*Oh, no. Oh, no. Oh, no. Please don't let it be about Joe Collins.*

"Remember my friend, Scarlett?" Liz asked.

Sofia let out a huge sigh of relief. "Yeah, what's up?"

"Well, today she got offered this huge book deal for writing about her real-life Iditarod adventures." Elizabeth Jane's voice warmed with pride, as if the accomplishment had been her own rather than that of a good friend.

"Whoa, that's huge. Congratulations!" Sofia could only imagine how ecstatic Scarlett must be. Although books weren't *her* thing, a big fashion deal was top of Sofia's dream list. It could change Sofia's entire life for the better. Actually, it could fix everything.

"Yeah, right? I'm really proud of her. Anyway, Lauren and I want to throw her a surprise party to celebrate and we were hoping you could help."

Crap. She wished life were simple enough to

accept an impromptu party invite, but no, she already had plans to take her dognapping career to the next level this weekend. Too late to turn back on that now.

She pretended to think it over, then made her voice suitably sad before answering with, "Umm... I'm busy Saturday."

Liz didn't give up. Instead, she just sounded happier. "Not Saturday. Tomorrow. Friday. You're not busy then, are you?"

Sofia's mind churned, but she just couldn't bring herself to lie to Liz yet again. "No," she said after admitting she truly had no other option.

Liz's satisfaction came through loud and clear. "Great, here's the plan..."

Sofia listened carefully as Liz revealed the details of her so-called "evil plan." If only she knew Sofia's other plans and how tame these were by comparison.

Sofia would need to brace herself for a very busy weekend ahead...

## Twenty-Six

The next evening, Scarlett and her two huskies came to Sofia's apartment for Wolfie's first ever doggie playdate. Sofia worried after the negative experience with Foxie that Wolfie wouldn't want to spend time with any other dogs, but the two lively sled dogs immediately brought him out of his shell.

No peeing or hiding under the table required.

Sofia invited Scarlett to sit with her at the table while the dogs ran loops around the living room.

"I have to admit, I didn't think you were ever going to call," the fair-haired Scarlett said as Sofia handed her a bottle of water from the fridge.

"What? Why not?" Sofia hadn't planned on calling, but she needed to act otherwise in order to carry out her part of the surprise.

The other girl shrugged and fixed her eyes on one of the many stains that now decorated the apartment's carpet. "Don't take this the wrong way, but I got the impression that you didn't like me very much. That maybe you don't like most people very much."

Sofia laughed. "You're right. I don't like most people, but you seem pretty okay."

"You know what? I'll take that." Scarlett raised her bottle in salute, and Sofia clinked the edge of her diet coke can against it.

"So, what have you been up to?" Sofia asked casually. She hated making small talk, given how much she had to do it every day for her job, but she also needed to keep Scarlett talking for at least an hour to give Liz and Lauren the time they needed to set up the surprise party.

A pink glow lit Scarlett's pale cheek. "Actually, something amazing happened just yesterday."

"Oh?" Sofia feigned surprise even though Elizabeth Jane had already told her the full details of Scarlett's six-figure book deal.

"Yeah, so earlier this year I self-published a memoir about my year as a musher. It was pretty short but laid out the important facts. Anyway, this big New York publisher came across it somehow and apparently fell in love. They asked me if I'd be interested in expanding my story and turning it into a three-book fiction series. I said *yes*!" Scarlett let out a big breath and sank back into the couch cushions, beaming at Sofia as she did.

"That's awesome. Congrats!" She patted Scarlett on the knee, even though she knew most women would hug under these circumstances. She couldn't act too out of the ordinary without giving away Elizabeth Jane's surprise, especially since Scarlett already seemed to have her figured out.

"Thanks. It still doesn't feel real."

"I bet. I know it's not the same thing, but I still remember when I sold my first dress to a stranger on Etsy. It was a big moment for me, and I only made forty bucks."

Scarlett nodded, a wistful smile on her face. "It never gets old, does it? Living the dream."

"You might be living it, but I'm still dreaming the dream." Sofia couldn't help but roll her eyes at that one. If she were living the dream, she wouldn't be living in this crappy Mountain View apartment complex and playing nice to strangers at the mall for little more than minimum wage.

"Ha!" Scarlett pulled both of her legs up beneath her so that she was now sitting crisscross applesauce. She seemed much more comfortable that way, too. "Are you a fan of *Les Mis,* too? I like the book so much better, but the musical was pretty good, too."

Sofia shrugged. She'd never been a fan of musicals or books, so didn't know what to tell her new acquaintance. Could she somehow become friends with Scarlett as a way of distancing herself from Blinky's gang? This evening felt forced, largely because it was, but maybe in the future...

Scarlett laughed again and crinkled the half-empty water bottle between her knees. "I'm guessing perhaps you're not. That's okay! Tell me, what do you like?"

Sofia didn't hesitate. "Fashion and animals, especially dogs. Not really into anything else."

"So I think, if you can find a way to combine those two passions into one thing, then you'll be living your dream, too. It's what happened with me, books, and sled dogs... and *bam!*"

Sofia had heard plenty about Scarlett from their shared friend and could now finally see why Liz found her so inspiring. Even if Sofia didn't much care for books, both women did love their dogs. Studying her more closely now, she also noted

Scarlett's well-tailored clothes and perfectly coordinated accessories. Their fashion tastes might not match up, but they both seemed to know the confidence-boosting power of finding the perfect outfit.

Sofia had already chosen to combine her dark aesthetic with fairytale inspiration. Adding yet another element to the mashup seemed like overkill. She wouldn't be caught dead in a cheetah print or any other animal skin for that matter. She pretended to think Scarlett's suggestion over before saying, "That's an interesting idea, but I'm anti-cruelty, so no furs for me."

But Scarlett was not easily discouraged. Now that she had an idea, she wanted to see it through. That kind of stick-to-it-iveness is what Sofia needed in her life.

Scarlett grinned, now talking with her hands. "Who says they have to be real? Or that they even have to be fur at all? What about taking colors, shapes, feelings, inspired by dogs and see what you come up with?"

Wow, why hadn't Sofia thought of this before? Oh, right, because she'd only just become a dog person less than two weeks ago. Still, Scarlett made a remarkable point...

"Hmmm... That's a good idea. I'll think about it and see what I come up with."

Her guest—and now mentor, apparently—nodded vigorously. "Yup. And when you're a famous designer with shows in Paris, Milan, and Tokyo, remember that I helped give you the idea and maybe give me a place in your next runway show."

Sofia laughed, but Scarlett regarded her with a serious expression.

"It's this bucket list thing my fiancé Henry and I have," she explained softly. "When we met, he had this list from his grandpa, and then we fell in love, we decided to make a new list together. One of my more ambitious items is to model in fashion show. But, hey, you can do anything if you set your mind to it. Just look at me and my book deal."

Sofia had to admit, Scarlett's enthusiasm was infectious.

What would life be like if she committed to her own decisions more?

Well, she would find out soon enough. Her big rescue now loomed less than twenty-four hours away.

# Twenty-Seven

After discussing dreams and aspirations for the next hour, Sofia found herself firmly in the pro-Scarlett camp. By the time Elizabeth Jane texted the all-clear, Sofia had already formed the perfect plan to deliver the guest of honor to her party.

"Hey, so do you have any books I can borrow to help me learn more about training this guy?" She hooked a thumb toward Wolfie who'd decided to take a break from playing to drain his water dish.

Scarlett's eyes grew wide. "Do I ever! At least ten or twelve. Maybe even more. How about we set a playdate for next week and I'll bring them to you then?"

Sofia crossed to the door and rummaged for her

keys. "Actually, I kind of need all the help I can get *now*. Do you mind if I follow you home now to grab at least a few to help get me started?"

"Sure! Looks like our doggos are getting worn out anyway." Scarlett stood, too, and stretched her arms overhead.

"Great, thank you."

Sofia refilled Wolfie's water dish, then took him for a quick pee break before following Scarlett back to her apartment complex.

When they stepped through the door, everyone jumped out to yell surprise. Scarlett's fiancé, Henry, lifted her into the air and spun her around before dropping her back into his arms for a kiss. It reminded Sofia a bit of the scene everyone loved from *Dirty Dancing*.

She'd never met Henry in person before but had seen many a news story about his billionaire bucket list challenge. Up close, his bi-colored eyes and posh mannerisms had her absolutely mesmerized. She couldn't stop staring as the couple shared this happy, effortless moment.

"Are you surprised?" Elizabeth Jane asked breathlessly, breaking Sofia's trance by taking first Scarlett then her in a hug.

"Uhh, yeah!" Scarlett squealed and did an excited

little hop. "I just got the deal yesterday. How did you even have time?"

"Lauren was a huge help!" Liz said as the tall, athletic brunette hugged Scarlett to her chest. "By the way, Sofia, this is Lauren Ramsey. So glad you two finally get to meet!"

"Hello!" Lauren extended her hand toward Sofia and gave it a firm shake. "I love your dress!"

Sofia did a small curtsy, showing off one of her latest designs. The energy in the room had her smiling from ear to ear. She almost forgot about her plans for the following night. That is, until another familiar face found hers.

A handsome pair of hazel eyes connected with hers across the room, and now that she'd been spotted, there was no getting away. Hunter excused himself from his conversation with Liz's fiancé Dorian, not removing his gaze from Sofia for even a second. It was just her luck that these two men knew each other. *Of course.* Anchorage PD wasn't that big, after all.

*So stupid!* She should have delivered Scarlett to the party, then hightailed it out of there. Seeing Hunter in person made it harder to resist him. She could risk everything for a man like that—everything except her Wolfie. She needed to be strong. She *would* be strong.

"Sofia, you look... well," Hunter said with a wink as he pulled her in for a hug.

"Thanks," she muttered as her entire body melted into his like butter. Apparently her brain had done a poor job communicating their new position on this man.

"Wait a sec." Elizabeth Jane looked from Sofia to Hunter and back again. "Do you two already know each other?"

"A little," Hunter said with a sly smile. "But definitely not as much as I'd like."

"Oh my gosh, Sofia!" Liz cried with a look of sheer delight splashed across her freckled face. "This is one of the hot cop friends I was telling you about."

Hunter hung his head and laughed. "Wait, this is who you and Dorian wanted to fix me up with tonight?"

Liz placed both hands on her hips, but it did not give her any added authority in this awkward situation. "Is that a problem?" she demanded, raising an eyebrow at Hunter.

He shrugged. "Well, we already went out before, but she blew me off partway through and then stopped taking my calls."

Sofia wanted to fade through the wall behind her and never return to this apartment—or this conversation. She glanced toward the door, but it had already been shut tight.

Liz huffed and jerked Sofia's arm. "You said you weren't seeing anyone!"

"I'm not *seeing* anyone," she argued. "I saw him one time and that was it."

"I don't get it. Why don't you like him? I figured you two would be a perfect match. That's why I wanted to make sure you'd both be here tonight."

"Liz, shut up. Please just stop," Sofia growled as Scarlett and Lauren watched with wide eyes.

"Wait. Actually, I'd like to know that, too," Hunter said, placing a hand on Elizabeth Jane's shoulder as the two of them stood united against Sofia, both demanding answers she would never willingly give. "Why *don't* you like me?"

"I..." *What can I possibly say?*

"C'mon, that's enough," Lauren said, putting two hands on Sofia's back to lead her away from the group and deeper into the party.

"Sorry about them," she whispered in Sofia's ear. "Liz and Scarlett tend to get a bit juvenile when they're together. I'm sure they didn't mean to embarrass you like that. I can create a distraction if you want to sneak out of here without them noticing."

Sofia had only just met Lauren, but already she'd become her favorite person in the entire world. "Please and thank you," she said as she calculated the quickest path to the door.

"You've got it!" Lauren ran back over to the group and said something with big, sweeping hand gestures that made the other two women double over with laughter.

Sofia saw her chance and grabbed it tight—slipping out of the apartment, racing down the hall, and...

Running straight into Hunter, who had also decided to mount an escape.

# Twenty-Eight

Sofia wanted to cry. This week just kept on getting worse and worse. The only thing worse that having to escape the company of a handsome man was getting caught in the process. And now here they were. Sofia's mortification knew no bounds.

Hunter, on the other hand, burst out laughing. "Looks like we can at least agree on one thing. That sucked."

"Yeah... well, bye." She needed to get out of there, get away from him. If rudeness was required, then so be it. She had no desire to make small talk.

Hunter followed her down the stairs, stopping midway. "Hey, hold on. You know that was embarrassing for me, too. Especially after you ghosted me like that."

"I didn't..." Although it was only natural to defend herself, Sofia needed to curtail that inclination real quick. She needed to make him go away without asking anymore questions.

"You're right," she said with what she hoped was a formidable scowl. "I'm not interested. Sorry if you find that embarrassing." Sofia glided down the stairs with more confidence then she felt, hoping that this would finally be the end of her messed-up saga with Hunter.

"Nope, you're not getting away that easily." Hunter trod after her with rapid footfalls. Was he trying to force her to physically run away from him?

Could she not escape this situation with the very last shred of her dignity intact? Sofia quickened her pace, but it was too late.

Hunter caught up to her and scooped Sofia into a fireman's carry.

"Hey, put me down!" she yelled.

"I will if you promise not to walk away from me again."

"No way, you can't just—"

"Okay, then I'll carry you." He took quick strides

down the sidewalk, delivering her to the apartment's courtyard but still refusing to let her go.

"Hunter, what are you doing? This is not okay."

"You know what else isn't okay? The way you've been lying to me and to yourself."

She looked up at him, their faces dangerously close, and for the first time, she saw the hurt reflecting in his eyes. That made what she needed to do even more difficult. "I haven't—"

"Yes, you have. I felt it then, and I know you did, too. In the factory, when we almost kissed. I feel it now, too."

This caught her off guard. She needed to fight, to demand he put her down, but instead she asked, "We almost kissed?"

He kept his hazel eyes fixed on her, pleading her to see something. Perhaps it was his earnestness, the fact he meant everything he said now, that he wouldn't let her get away without first giving him a proper chance. "Contrary to me carrying you around like a crazed gorilla right now, I'm actually a really decent guy. You'd know that if you gave me a chance."

"But I..."

"But what?"

"I don't know." D*on't you understand? Can't you see this is hard for me, too? Please just let me go.*

"Well, then, that makes two of us." He plopped her down onto the pavement and sighed.

Sofia stepped closer, but Hunter wouldn't meet her eyes. "I'm sorry. I didn't mean to hurt you. I'm just... well, I'm really messed up."

He let out a sad chuckle and shook his head, still avoiding her gaze. She hated that she'd hurt him like this, but what other choice did she have then? Have now?

"That's the thing, Sofia. *We all are.* Every single one of us. Even me."

Sofia shook her head and placed her hand on Hunter's arm. "Not you. You're perfect."

He laughed bitterly. "Making fun of me now?"

She bit her lip. This was not going well. "I had no idea you liked me so much. I wouldn't have ever agreed to go out with you if I knew..."

"Knew what?" At last his gaze zipped toward hers. Its intensity caused her breath to catch in her throat. She didn't have the answers he wanted. She didn't have any she could offer.

"You know what *I* know? I know that our feelings are mutual. I know that we could be so great together, Sofia. Even our friends know that, which explains the most awkward fixup in the history of mankind back there. Everyone wants us together— the whole universe, even—everyone but *you*. And no matter how hard I try, I just can't understand why."

She shook her head, holding back her tears. If Hunter saw her cry, this would all be over. Then what would happen to Wolfie? To the other dogs who needed her? "I'm not right for you, Hunter."

He placed a gentle hand on her wrist, reminding her of how close they now stood. All she needed to do was turn around and walk away, but somehow she couldn't bring herself to budge. Not now. Not yet.

"Won't you give me the chance to decide that for myself?" Hunter pleaded.

Tears continued to sting the corners of her eyes, but she refused to let them fall. She hated to hurt Hunter like this, but it was better to do it now than to let him continue this inconvenient infatuation. "I..."

"Hey!" A high-pitched voice floated down from above, breaking through the bubble of intensity that surrounded them. "Hey, Sofia Stepanov!"

Sofia snapped her head up and saw a pair of familiar girls leaning over the edge of the roof.

"Celeste?" she asked, recognizing the former mean girl's red locks even in the waning light.

"Yeah! Allie from school is here, too. Come up and say hi!" The other girl waved, then collapsed into laughter. Yes, that was Allie Mayfair, all right. Sofia hadn't realized the two had become friends again after what she'd done to split them apart and get her revenge for all the hurt they'd caused her.

Her heart picked up its pace. Did they know? Of course they couldn't know. Sofia had never told a soul, which is why her plan had worked so well.

Normally, these two high school enemies would be the last people she'd want to spend any time with, but tonight there was a different person who bottomed out her list...

She took the stairs two at a time to put as much distance between herself and Hunter as she could. Hopefully, when she looked back, he would finally be gone.

# Twenty-Nine

R ooftop terraces were somewhat of a rarity in Anchorage, given the huge amounts of snow that blanketed the city for the better part of the year. As she ascended several flights of stairs to reach the roof, Sofia briefly wondered how much Scarlett must be paying for rent to afford a place with such nice amenities. However, these trivial thoughts fled when she reached the top of the building and came face to face with her former tormenters.

Celeste spotted her instantly and ran over for a hug.

Allie hung back, leaning against the half wall and nursing an over-filled glass of wine.

Sofia flinched. Her muscle memory from more

than ten years ago had remained intact, and her poor body expected to be slapped, spit on, or worse.

"So glad to see you again." Celeste offered a kind smile and hugged Sofia a second time. She seemed to have grown up quite a bit over the years.

But still...

It was too little, too late. A childhood full of memories stampeded through Sofia's head. The rumors, the taunts, the sometimes physical abuse. Her parents had told Sofia to stand up for herself, that if the bullies respected her they would stop picking on her—but they had been very, very wrong.

Day after day, the mean girls made her life a hell. Celeste and Allie were their queens, two inseparable best friends whose first priority was maintaining their hard-won throne of popularity.

Nothing Sofia tried could dampen their cruelty. Not until she came up with *the plan*. The plan had worked like a charm, and for months, Sofia had been on top of the world, free from harassment, free to enjoy the remainder of her high school days.

Until the worst happened...

"How's your daughter?" Sofia asked, remembering how she felt when she'd first heard the news of Allie's pregnancy. Her little girl must be at least twelve by now. Hardly a little girl at all. And to think

Sofia was partially to blame for her existence. For this mess that Allie had now become. Allie and Celeste may have made her childhood a hell, but Sofia's actions had ruined the rest of their lives—or at least Allie's.

Allie shrugged and took another long drink from her wine goblet. "Milly is fine. She's with my parents tonight."

"Oh, that's good." How much did she have to say before she could mount another escape? She certainly couldn't say what she most wanted—that she was sorry. "And h-how is everything else?" she said instead.

"Good as it can be for a high school dropout," Allie grumbled into her drink.

"She's being modest," Celeste said, walking with Sofia over to the wall. "She just got a promotion at work."

"Head tour guide, whoopie." Allie pumped her fist in the air, slightly losing her footing. She clutched to the wall and took another drink.

Celeste raised her voice and furrowed her brow. "Stop putting yourself down, Al. It is a big deal! Think of the difference you're making, the awareness you're spreading."

"The people I'm entertaining? Yeah, yeah, I get

it." Allie let out a long sigh, then frowned at her now empty glass.

Sofia felt trapped between the two friends, each growing increasingly hostile toward the other right before her eyes. *She* had done this. *Sofia*. Her actions all those years ago still held tight to their lives like burrs to a hemline.

"Congratulations on your promotion, Allie. Where do you work?" Sofia asked, drawing both sets of eyes to herself.

"The Wolf Sanctuary up in Eagle River. I show the tourists around." She shrugged. "No big deal."

"We ran into each other again a couple years back when I was called in to take some photos for their new website," Celeste explained.

"And it's just like old times. Isn't it, C?" Allie swore and stamped her foot.

Celeste scowled. "Yeah, I guess some people never change. C'mon, Sofia. This one's obviously had too much to drink. Her inner wicked witch is showing."

Sofia allowed Celeste to lead her away, but the physical distance from Allie didn't dampen the emotional impact Sofia had had on the girl's life.

*Still.* All these years later.

Would it be like that again with Joe Collins and

Hunter and all the other people she'd hurt by trying to do something good? She'd attempted to mete out justice before and look at what had happened. Sofia had the power to destroy lives, whether or not it's what she wanted.

The thought of Hunter becoming broken and bitter like Allie devastated Sofia.

"Oh, look," Celeste said, pointing across the roof to an attractive couple poised on a wicker lounger with a small group gathered before them. "Did you know Scarlett has celebrity friends? That's Lolly Winston."

Sofia squinted in the direction Celeste had pointed but didn't recognize the woman she saw flanked on one side by her husband and the other, Liz. "I'm sorry, who?"

"Lolly Winston. She's basically the Christina Aguilera of our generation. Don't you listen to the radio?" Celeste laughed and dragged Sofia over to the unknown singer. *Why is she acting like we're such good friends? Does she know?*

Liz and Lolly both stared down at the tiny screen in Liz's hands.

"And this is Delilah after her bath," Liz declared with an obvious maternal pride before swiping again. "This is Delilah with her favorite stuffed bunny... Oh, and this is Delilah getting ready for bedtime."

"Let me see that," Lolly's husband said, gesturing for the phone.

"That's Oscar Rockwell," Celeste whispered into her ear. "Isn't he hot? He's not famous or anything, but he does run this huge rescue organization for sled dogs. I think that's how Scarlett knows them."

"Is Delilah a Chow Chow?" Oscar asked Liz.

Sofia held her breath, praying she could stop time, wind it backward, undo it all.

Liz nodded enthusiastically and took her phone back from Oscar. "Yeah, isn't she the cutest? I just love her little scrunched face."

"She's beautiful," the vet agreed, but a frown now filled his face. "Where did you get her?"

"My friend found her wandering the streets in a storm."

"That's what I thought. Tell me..." Oscar nodded and pressed a few keys on his phone then pushed it toward Liz. "Is this her?"

"What? Oh my gosh!" Liz searched the crowd on the rooftop until her eyes landed on Sofia. "There's my friend who found her! Sofia, look! Delilah's real name is Fanta, and her owner's been trying to find her."

*No, no, no, no!* This particular truth had finally caught up to Sofia. How she prayed the others would remain hidden in her past.

Liz's eyes searched Sofia's for answers. Her face fell. Sofia watched as her friend's heart broke right in front of her.

There was nothing left to do except run away and refuse to look back.

# Thirty

The facts against Sofia stacked up like an unsteady Jenga tower. One wrong move and the whole thing would come toppling over, creating a giant mess she'd never be able to clean up.

Joe Collins had seen her car. He knew his dog had been stolen.

Liz had just informed the party that Sofia was the one who brought the dog to her.

And at least one person would be able to fit these pieces together and solve the puzzle—*Hunter Burke.*

"I have to go get some air," Sofia mumbled before pushing her way through the crowd and away from her friend. She couldn't bring herself to confront the hurt in Liz's face, in her voice. Even if she hadn't yet figured out what Sofia had done, she would soon enough. Liz already loved the Chow like a second child, and now it would be taken away.

She'd lose her baby—and all because of Sofia.

"Get some air?" a man asked as she swept by. "You do realize you're already outside, don't you?"

*Hunter.* Of course this night would get worse still. It's what she deserved.

"You look like you're going to be sick," he called after her.

Sofia quickened her pace until at last she reached the stairs. Unfortunately, Hunter had followed her. She couldn't very well lead him back to her car.

Not now. Now with the revelation about the stolen dog so fresh in the air.

"Wait." Hunter jogged down the stairs after her. "At least let me drive you home. I promise I won't get mad if you puke in my car."

What choice did she have? She could lead him to her car, the same one placed at the scene of her crime by Joe Collins. Or she could go back to the party and face what she had done to Liz—or to Allie, for that matter.

Or...

In this case, Hunter really was the lesser evil. She felt her resolve crumble and blow away in the light evening breezes. With a sigh, she stopped walking and asked, "Do you promise to take me straight home?"

"I promise." Hunter smiled so large that all his teeth showed. Why did he like her so much? How could he not see that she was damaged goods?

"And you won't try to invite yourself in?"

He raised his hand in a scout's salute. "On my honor."

*You don't have any other choices here*, she reminded herself. *Hunter will drive you home and you will do everything you can not to fall for him again. Be distant, cold, cruel. Just don't let him see the effect he has on you.*

Her internal pep talk complete, she sighed and met Hunter's gaze of boyish anticipation. "Okay. Fine," she said.

Hunter placed a hand on the small of her back and guided her toward the parking lot. "Such a grateful princess thanking the brave knight for her rescue."

Sofia twisted to the side to escape his touch, and Hunter laughed.

"Relax, I've known you long enough to know you're not a princess. At least not the fairytale kind."

"Gee, thanks," she grumbled. Maddeningly, she

still wanted Hunter to like her. She enjoyed knowing that he found her worthy of his attentions... but he didn't know the full truth about her. Once he did, that sparkle in his eyes would be gone forever. Until then, Sofia needed to be strong, to hope she could hide her secrets tonight and then avoid accidentally running into the charming cop all the nights that came after.

Hunter called her out instantly. "You can't decide whether or not you're a princess. You're sending off mixed signals left and right. How's a guy supposed to keep up?"

"He's supposed to stop trying." She smiled despite herself, but luckily Hunter didn't seem to notice as he led the way over to a small truck.

"This is me. Hop in."

At least they wouldn't be riding in the cruiser this time. That would have done Sofia in for sure.

"You seem sick a lot," Hunter said as they both buckled in. "Maybe you should see a doctor."

"I'll be fine." She laid her head against the cool glass of the window. Maybe she would throw up before the night was through.

"Is it a nervous thing, or do you have some horrible infectious disease I should know about?"

Hunter backed his truck out of the parking lot, and they were on their way.

Sofia began counting down the minutes back to her apartment. Not long now and this night would be over. Tomorrow would also be horrible, but then she could finally be free. Go back to normal. Whatever that was...

"I don't want to talk about it," she said when she felt his eyes on her.

"Yeah, you don't much care for talking. I noticed when you ran away. Been doing a lot of that lately, too, huh? What does that make, three times in one night?"

Accepting a ride from Hunter had been a huge mistake. She should have walked, even if it took her all night to reach home. She groaned. "What do you want, Hunter?"

"I already told you what I want. *A chance.*"

She closed her eyes and sighed. "And *I* already told *you,* I'm messed up and not looking for a relationship."

"You keep saying that, but I also know this isn't the real you. I've met that person, and she's incredible. She's the one I want to get to know."

"She's dead," Sofia answered flatly. "Or at least in a very serious coma."

"Might she be revived by true love's kiss?"

She opened her eyes and found Hunter staring at her once again—definitely not the safest when it came to driving.

"I don't know, but I'll ask my dog when I get home."

He laughed. "You never run out of comebacks, do you?"

"And you never run out of lines," she shot back.

"Then it seems we both have each other figured out."

"Seems that way."

They drove the rest of the way in a tensely charged silence. When at last they reached Sofia's apartment complex, she grabbed the door handle before Hunter even had a chance to park.

But he stopped her from exiting by placing a firm hand on her shoulder, sending a tingling sensation right through her. Why was it such a challenge to get her mind and heart on the same page?

"I'm not giving up on you. If you ever change your mind about me, I'm just a phone call away."

Sofia nodded, mumbled her thanks, then crept away into the night.

Why was it that Hunter refused to give up on her, but she'd already long since given up on herself?

## Thirty-One

An unexpected call from her boss awakened Sofia the next morning. She almost refused to answer. After all, this was supposed to be her day off. And after the night she'd had and what was planned for this evening, there was no way she could cover a shift--even if the store owner begged and offered her holiday pay.

Sofia forced a cough after putting the phone on speaker. "I can't come into work today, Jean. I'm not feeling great."

"Yeah, and I'm not doing too great, either." Jean sighed before continuing at an agonizing slow pace. "Sofia... did you know... that your registers... were more than... two hundred dollars off this week?"

"What? No, I didn't," Sofia answered honestly. She'd just woken up and already she had a migraine.

Jean took a deep, shaky breath on the other end of the line. "There are holes... in our inventory, too."

This Sofia did know—and she hated herself for it, especially since she simply couldn't admit the truth. "I have no idea what happened. I promise I didn't steal from you."

"Well, I know *you* wouldn't steal," Jean said all in one breath before going back to her broken way of speaking. "But somebody certainly... is. Have you... spotted any... suspicious shoppers lately? Anything... out of the ordinary that... I should know about?"

Sofia shook her head furiously and prayed Jean wouldn't review the security footage. "No," she insisted, perhaps too adamantly. "Honestly, there haven't been that many shoppers at all."

Jean let out another beleaguered sigh. "Yes, I know... that, too... I hate to say this..." She sighed yet again. "But you may need... to start looking for another job... I can't keep... running at a loss."

"No!" Sofia was startled by the passion in her own voice. Wolfie lifted his head from his paws and tilted his head in confusion. "Don't give up yet," she continued. "I'll keep an extra careful watch on the store. I'll put in unpaid overtime. I'll find a way to keep things going."

"I appreciate your... dedication... Sofia. Really, I do... But there might not be... anything we can do.... The mall has been... collapsing... in on itself for years... Everyone shops... online now."

Sofia rubbed little circles into her temples, desperately hoping she could coax out a plan to fix everything. "You might be right, but we at least have to try."

Jean sighed at least three more times before saying goodbye, and with each resigned expulsion of air, Sofia felt her conviction grow. Things had gotten even worse than she'd anticipated. Her choices were now beginning to take choices away from others. What would Jean do without her store? Sofia had passively watched from the corner as Preeti stole hundreds in merchandise and had apparently also weaseled cash from the register. Jean shouldn't be the one to pay the price of keeping Sofia's secrets.

*None* of this was fair.

Sofia had to find a way to set things right and, unfortunately, that would require something she had very little of.

*Money.*

She now had "lost" inventory to replace, a large

wolf hybrid to care for, and an unknown number of additional rescues coming her way later that night. She still wanted to repay the pet store for the supplies Blinky had stolen on her behalf, too.

But her Etsy sales had all but dried up. She wasn't even covering the cost of materials anymore. If only she had some way of making quick cash, then she could fix everything.

She stayed in bed for a very long time, weighing her various options. In the end, only one made any sense at all.

But it scared her senseless. Still, she had to find a way to justify it to herself and then take the plunge. No other options existed. Not anymore.

Pulling herself to a sitting position, she patted the bed so that Wolfie would jump up and cuddle beside her.

"Good boy," she said as she hugged him around the neck. "I did a good thing by saving you, right?"

Wolfie licked her face, covering it with a fresh sheen of doggie slime. His tail thumped merrily on the mattress.

"I love you, too, boy." Sofia laughed, but the mood still felt heavy. "Wolfie?" she ventured. "If something will happen no matter what... Like if someone will do wrong with or without your involvement… but getting involved yourself means you have power you wouldn't have had, power to do something good… then is it really so wrong for you to intervene?"

Wolfie didn't understand. Sofia hardly understood herself.

She tried to explain it a different way. "People will buy them one way or another. If I sell, then I'll have the money I need to pay back Jean and the pet store and to help the other dogs. If I don't sell, then I won't be able to help. So, what's the greater crime? If I act, I can help those people and dogs. If I don't, then I can't. Don't you get it?"

Wolfie barked to show his support.

"Good boy! So, you do understand…"

She gave her canine companion another warm hug.

"You understand exactly why I need to sell drugs."

## Thirty-Two

U nable to wait even a second longer, Sofia wound up at the Ridge well before anyone else in the group. Apparently being fashionably early wasn't really fashionable at all. But waiting at the bar eased her anxiety somewhat. It was better to be here than pacing around her apartment.

Finally, at five past eight, D-Man joined Sofia in her waiting. "I hope that's nothing too strong." He took a seat beside her at the counter and gestured for the bartender. "Going to need your head on straight for what comes later... Yeah, one Bud Light, please."

She stared into the bright red liquid lining her glass and shrugged. "You can relax. It's just a Shirley Temple."

"Virgin, eh?" His cue ball scalp turned pink as he smiled.

"One-hundred percent," Sofia said before taking an exaggerated sip from her mocktail. She'd always ordered Diet Coke at bars before, but Hunter had gotten her hooked on Temples at the Miners Pub.

Had that really only been a week ago? It felt like an entire lifetime. So much had changed, including Sofia herself. Which reminded her...

"I have a favor to ask," she said as the bartender slid a tall glass of foamy lager Matt's way.

He wrapped both hands around the pint and grinned at Sofia. "What's up?"

"I need money."

He raised an eyebrow but didn't actually seem all that surprised. "So, you need a job?"

The air hung thick around them. What if he said no? Sofia would truly have no options left. She needed this. Needed Matt to understand. "*Please*."

He leaned back in his chair and kicked his heels against its legs. "Let's see how tonight goes first. I'd hate to think I'm a bad influence on you."

"Well, you can't corrupt the already corrupted," she said with a frown. "I'm looking forward to tonight being over."

D-Man took several large gulps from his beer and

shuddered. "It'll get worse before it gets better. When you see the dogs..."

"No, I don't want to hear about it."

"You're going to see it, though, unless you plan to do the whole thing with your eyes closed."

"Who knows? Maybe I will," she answered, draining the rest of her drink and wishing for maybe the first time ever that she'd ordered something with a little liquid courage swirled into the mix.

Sofia ordered another Shirley Temple, and they sat nursing their drinks in silence for the next several minutes.

"Blinky! Pretty! Over here!" D-Man waved his friends over and greeted them happily. Sofia, on the other hand, felt like a venomous snake ready to uncoil and sink her fangs straight into Preeti. She hadn't liked helping her steal clothes, but for this girl she hardly knew to steal from her register as well? Yup, that brought out the mama snake in her.

"I have to go to the bathroom," she muttered, slipping off the stool and slithering away. When she returned from the powder room, the rest of the group had arrived and grabbed a pair of tables in the back of the tavern. Sofia squeezed in beside Matt and tried not to wince as he stuck his arm around her. Part of their plan involved making the others think they had become an actual item. That would make it easier to leave unchallenged when the time came to infiltrate the fighting ring.

"Missed you," he said, giving her a wet kiss on the cheek.

"Aww, so cute!" Preeti trilled.

"So elementary school!" Blinky scoffed. "What's next, holding hands?"

D-Man grabbed Sofia's hand and laced his fingers between hers, waving their joined fists back and forth for all to see.

"Ridiculous," Blinky grumbled with an eye roll that ended in a twitching spasm.

As the night wore on, Sofia became thankful for the constant contact with Matt. Holding his hand kept her focused, kept her nerves in check. A couple hours later, he brought his face close to her ear and whispered, "It's time. Are you ready?"

Sofia squeezed his hand in confirmation, and a moment later, both of them were standing on their feet before the group.

"Me and my lady are going to head somewhere more private. See you lugs later."

They both mumbled their goodbyes and took off into the dark night. D-Man had helped retrieve her car from Scarlett's apartment complex earlier that afternoon, but now she needed to abandon it again and drive with her partner in crime to their pickup location.

First the cargo vans, then the dogs.

"Where'd you park the vans?" she asked after they'd shut their doors and settled into Matt's musty sedan.

"Not far from here. By a U-Haul store. Shouldn't take us more than five minutes to get there."

They didn't say much more as they drove toward the rally point. Matt's nerves seemed to be every bit as frazzled as her own. Neither would feel better until they'd finished their mission and delivered the dogs safe and sound to the old textile factory holding ground.

Sofia's heartbeat quickened as she spotted a pair of headlights following them out of the Ridge's parking lot. D-Man must have seen it, too, because he took several more turns than were needed to reach their location.

Still, it wasn't enough.

When they parked, the other car parked with them. And Preeti emerged from the driver's seat with a triumphant smirk. "I knew you two were full of crap. Now tell me what's really going on."

# Thirty-Three

S ofia wanted to scream. Preeti's ambush was *not* part of the plan. They hadn't even begun the rescue and already it had gotten mucked up.

"I'm not going away until you tell me why you're creeping around like a couple of characters from *Scooby Doo*," Preeti said as she crossed her arms and stared both of them down.

"Preeti, go away. Seriously, get out of here," D-Man hissed.

But the caramel-skinned girl dug her heels in with a dramatic huff. "No way! If you're going to have some fun, I want to be a part of it, too. So stop holding out on me and cough up the deets."

D-Man glanced toward Sofia, who glowered at Preeti.

"Not going to spit it out? Well, fine, that's just fine." Preeti pulled a lighter and a pack of cigarettes from her purse and shook one out.

Nobody said anything as she lit the Marlboro and lifted it to her lips.

"You want to wait? I've got all night, but it seems like *you* have someplace to be, and it isn't some roach-infested love nest, so don't try to pull that one over on me again. You may have fooled the others, but not me."

"What is wrong with you?" Sofia blurted out, unable to control her mounting rage for even a moment longer. She thought of Jean's call earlier that morning, of Preeti greedily stuffing stolen garments into her bag, of her standing between them and the dogs who needed to be rescued now.

Preeti simply smiled between slow drags on her cigarette.

"Do you even know what you're doing? Do you know who you're hurting?" Sofia clenched her fists at her sides, and it took all her muster to keep them there.

"No, and that's the point. I won't know until you tell me." Preeti spoke slowly as if Sofia were her intellectual inferior, all the while wearing her hideous grin.

Sofia couldn't remember ever hating anyone this intensely. Not even Celeste and Allie back in her school days when she'd been little more than a victim. Well, Sofia was all grown up now, and unwilling to stand for anyone's crap. She'd had more than enough now. Sofia grabbed the burning cigarette from Preeti's fingers and stomped it into the ground.

"Hey, that wasn't cool!" Preeti had murder in her eyes that Sofia was sure matched her own.

D-Man thrust himself between the two women, placing a hand on each of their shoulders. "Both of you, stop. Just stop!" Turning to Preeti, he said, "If I tell you, then you're a part of this, too. You have to help and you can't tell a soul. Not even Blinky."

Preeti nodded, and the greed of the forthcoming knowledge flashed in her charcoal eyes.

D-Man took a step back and recounted his discovery of the fighting ring with none of the tears or shortness of breath that had punctuated his words when he first shared it with Sofia.

"So, you see..." he concluded, "we have to rescue them, and since you just *had to know*, now you're a part of this, too. So, are you girls ready?"

Preeti shrugged, seeming to be completely unaffected by the plight of the dogs or the risk of the mission that lay ahead. "Sounds more fun than wasting the rest of the night at the Ridge. Let's do this."

"Okay, good." Matt tossed a pair or keys to Preeti, who caught them in one fist. "Sofia and I will take the lead. You take up the rear. It's about ten minutes from here. I'll explain the rest once we're inside."

Preeti had the audacity to laugh as she spun the keychain around her index finger. "This will definitely be more fun than the Ridge. Ready when you are."

Matt nodded, and Sofia followed him into the waiting van. There would be no turning back now...

It was time to save some dogs.

# Thirty-Four

The twin vans pulled up to the old strip mall on Eureka. A vacant storefront sat between a dry cleaner's and a nail salon. Not a single light illuminated the parking lot as Sofia and her two accomplices clambered out into the open air.

"Didn't this place used to be a laundromat?" Preeti's voice shot into the night like a siren. For being a seasoned criminal, she sure struggled to keep a low profile.

Sofia groaned.

D-Man said, "Shut up and take a big, long breath of fresh air while you still can. You're not going to want to once you get inside." He fiddled with the lock until it popped open, and the three of them stepped inside.

Immediately, the aforementioned stench hit Sofia hard in the lungs—a vile combination of excrement, sweat, and blood.

"Gross," Preeti hissed, drawing the *S* sound out way too far. "Do they not take the dogs outside to use the bathroom?"

Sofia stared at her in disbelief. Could she really be this dense?

"It's not like they're pets," D-Man answered with far more patience than Sofia had remaining. He jerked the flashlight around the room, which agitated many of the dogs. Some barked, some yipped, others growled, but soon all contributed to a sizable ruckus.

And it would get them caught if they didn't hurry.

"We have to work fast!" Sofia urged the others. Her voice was barely discernible in all the noise.

"No way, I'm not getting bit!" Preeti argued, falling back a couple steps.

Matt pushed her aside and charged toward the wall of cages. "It's a risk we have to take. If you can't handle it, go keep watch outside.

When Preeti didn't budge, Matt thrust his bag of supplies into her chest. "Fine, you can hold my bag."

He rummaged inside until he found a leash and the first of many Slim Jims he'd filched from some gas station. "Sofia, you get one, too. Preeti, stay out of our way."

Preeti glowered at them both but kept hold of the bag while Sofia extracted a Slim Jim and a pair of heavy working gloves to protect her hands.

"Ready." She nodded at D-Man, and together they crept toward the cages.

"Start with the ones that are whimpering instead of barking or growling," she suggested. "They're less likely to attack. Maybe they can set a good example for the others."

"Yeah, you're right." D-Man unwrapped the Slim Jim and held it with shaky gloved hands. He took a deep breath and shook out his limbs before turning back to Sofia.

"Okay, so when we open the cage, I'll distract him with the meat and you loop the leash over his head. Easy, right?" His voice quavered just as Sofia's stomach did a somersault.

"Which one are we starting with?"

She followed the direction of Matt's outstretched arm, and for the first time, she shifted her gaze toward the dogs. Most of them were packed so tightly into their cages that they couldn't even stand.

Crates were stacked one on top of the other, allowing feces and urine to drip from the upper cages down into the fur of the dogs below. Open wounds attracted buzzing flies. Some had minor scrapes and others were missing chunks of muscle, ear, or muzzle.

"They left these dogs to die," Sofia choked out, zeroing in on their first rescue, a small, fluffy thing that had no business being mixed in—let alone fighting—the much larger dogs that surrounded it.

"No, they didn't leave them," Matt growled as Sofia twisted the lasso leash in her hands. "They'll be back to watch—and to bet money. Now c'mon, I'm going to open this one. Ready?"

"Yes," Sofia said, wiping away tears. She couldn't cry, couldn't compromise her vision or anything else about this important mission. These dogs needed her.

D-Man unhinged the cage and held the door in place with his body, only allowing a few inches of open space for the dog to stick its head out and sniff for the meat. Luckily, the extreme hunger seemed to outweigh any fear or aggression. Maybe somehow the dog knew that Sofia and Matt were different from the other humans he'd come across before.

Although Sofia was afraid of getting bitten, she

was more afraid of failing. She bravely stepped forward and dropped the leash over the poor dog's head, then gave it a firm tug. She held out another Slim Jim, and once the dog jumped down from its cage at the top of the stack, led it toward the waiting vans.

"It's okay," she spoke softly to the dog as they walked briskly away from its former prison. "You're safe now. I promise."

After shutting the petite husky mix into one of the waiting cages, Sofia returned to the inside.

Preeti had drawn closer to the dogs now, a look of horror marred her normally arrogant face. "What happened to these dogs?" she whispered. "It's so awful."

"People happened," Sofia said with a frown. "Bad people."

"Ready for the next one?" D-Man called.

"I'll do it!" Preeti insisted, pushing the bag of supplies at Sofia.

Sofia followed closely just in case the other girl lost her nerve again. This was a two-person job at minimum, and she'd hate for Matt to be caught without help.

Sure enough, Preeti froze when D-Man opened a

cage that housed what appeared to be a half-grown, fully terrified Pitbull puppy.

"C'mon! I can't hold him back forever. Once he finishes the meat, there's nothing to stop him from attacking us."

Preeti shook so violently Sofia could see the tremor without the aid of her flashlight. "I-I-I-I I can't!"

"*Move*," Sofia growled, pushing the supplies at their otherwise useless accomplice once more. When she turned around with the second dog in tow, she saw the backpack laying discarded on the ground with Preeti no place to be found.

Until she and the dog broke into the night air together. Sofia realized then that this young dog may have never seen the world outside those four walls before. This thought made her even more determined to save and rehabilitate every single one of these dogs.

"Help me!" she called to Preeti, motioning to the van with her chin.

Preeti continued to shake. "N-N-N-No. I'll just k-k-keep watch. Like D-Man s-s-said."

"Useless," Sofia muttered, crating the dog and returning to help D-Man inside.

Preeti finally brought her shivering under control

around the time Sofia emerged with their fifth rescue. Each dog was bigger and angrier than the last, but so far both Matt and Sofia had managed to avoid getting bitten. Somehow these dogs knew that whatever lay ahead had to be better than what was behind.

As Sofia coaxed the sixth dog into the last open crate in the first of the two vans, Preeti moved to a wooden bench outside of the salon next door. By dog number seven, she'd relaxed enough to bring out her cigarette and take long, luxurious drags while the others worked themselves to exhaustion in their mission to help the dogs.

Still, D-Man and Sofia persisted, not even losing speed despite their aching muscles and labored breathing. Sofia had just brought their ninth dog through the open door when the sound of sirens wailed in the distance.

"We have to go! Now!" Preeti jumped up from the bench and got behind the wheel of the van she'd driven earlier that night, the one that was already full of dogs. Of course, she had no idea where to go—Matt hadn't yet revealed the second half of the plan—but that didn't stop Preeti from peeling off into the night.

"Matt, c'mon!" Sofia shoved the leashed animal

into the back of the van without even bothering to crate him and called into the building which had almost been entirely emptied of dogs. Almost, but not quite.

D-Man ran out carrying the last of the supplies and jumped behind the wheel so they, too, could get away in time. About a mile and a half down, they passed a nasty traffic accident.

"They weren't coming for us," Sofia said with a relieved sigh. "Matt, we have to go back and get the others."

He shook his head and twitched so hard, he looked like the other Matt—like Blinky. "It's too late now. They're too close."

"But— "

"At least we were able to save the others."

D-Man drove them to the textile factory while Sofia furiously texted Preeti using his phone. They still owed these dogs more. Nobody was out of the woods yet.

# Thirty-Five

A fter finally tracking down Preeti and getting all the dogs safely crated and fed in the abandoned textile factory, Sofia came home and fell into bed. They could plan the rest of it tomorrow. First, she needed to sleep before her brain and body entirely shut down on her—and without her consent.

Cries from Wolfie the next morning rousted her from a fitful sleep. She'd tossed and turned with nightmares, flashbacks, and fears that felt almost like premonitions, but she did not wake until Wolfie nudged her with his wet nose and whimpered directly in her ear.

"I'm sorry, boy," Sofia said around a yawn. "Let's go outside."

Because she hadn't taken Wolfie out for a potty break after coming home the previous evening, he had to go—and go bad. She walked him around the building a few extra times to make up for this failure as a dog owner, then together they went back inside. The sun already hung high overhead, and Sofia found herself thankful that night had already completely disappeared from the sky. After all, it was during the night that all her most gruesome experiences seemed to take place.

Back inside, she reluctantly collected her phone and took a deep breath. She'd powered it off before the rescue. And even though she knew she should check for any messages, Sofia was terrified of the texts that would be waiting for her when she booted back up.

Wolfie laid his head in her lap for support and stared up at her with the huge amber eyes that always broke and healed her heart at the exact same time.

"Okay, I guess we have to find out sooner or later," she told him before letting out a slow, shaky breath and pushing down on the power button.

No cops had shown up at her door, so the news couldn't be too bad...

Right?

The list of notifications on her phone seemed to

scroll down forever. Most were from Liz, demanding answers and telling Sofia how much she'd hurt her. D-Man had also texted, but all he said was "call me." He'd sent the same identical text at least half a dozen times and left a few voicemails as well.

Choosing the only slightly less horrifying situation to confront first, she dialed D-Man's number and put the phone up to her ear.

He answered on the first ring. "Where have you been? I've been trying to get a hold of you for hours!"

"Sorry, I slept in." She yawned again to prove her point. A newfound terror had already coiled in her gut as she waited to find out the reason for Matt's many calls that morning.

"We need to make a plan for the dogs, and we need to make one fast," he said in a rushed whisper.

"I thought we had time to rehabilitate them and find good homes—"

Matt cut her off. "Not now," he said. He seemed angry, even though she hadn't done a single thing wrong. In fact, she'd risked a lot to help him. "They have every cop in the city on this after what happened last night," he continued with an exasperated sigh.

"The rescue?" Sofia locked eyes with Wolfie

again, hoping she would find strength in his under-standing pools of honey.

D-Man groaned, as if she should already know all that he still needed to reveal. "The fire."

This revelation surprised her. "Fire?"

"Yes, one they plan on ruling as arson." She thought back to Preeti and her cigarettes. There was simply no way...

"But we didn't—"

"It started minutes after we left. There was no one else there that night. They know someone broke into the laundromat, and it's only a matter of time before they figure out it was us. They're going to pin the fire on us, too."

Preeti had smothered her cigarette before driving away, hadn't she? Sofia pictured the wooden bench outside the nail salon, the one Preeti had sat on while chain-smoking last night. Surely, she couldn't have...

Sofia's brain shut down on her. The cause of the fire wasn't what mattered here. "But the dogs we didn't have time to save. Did they...?" She swallowed down the bile rising in her throat. Those poor, poor dogs.

"No, that's all over the news report, too. It's made people even angrier." Matt's voice shook with a barely controlled fury. She'd never heard him like this before. Did he somehow blame her for what had happened?

"The fire also did quite a bit of damage to the dry cleaner's and nail salon," he continued coldly. "Apparently all those chemicals made it burn faster and get out of control quicker."

Sofia let out a strangled sob. "So what are we going to do?"

"We need to move those dogs. *Now.*"

"But where? How?" She racked her brain but came up short. The only place that had enough room was Liz's ranch, and she couldn't put her friend at risk again—that is, if Liz even still was her friend now.

Matt's voice took on a panicked edge as he stumbled over his words. "I don't know. Maybe we can drive them out of the city and leave them in a field or something."

"What? You can't possibly be serious!"

Normally when Sofia raised her voice, Wolfie dove under the table for safety. But this time, he walked straight over to her and laid his head in her lap so she could stroke his soft fur. Her tears fell freely, mottling Wolfie's coat.

"Sofia, listen to me," D-Man said, at last with a small measure of kindness. "We haven't got a choice anymore. If we get picked up for arson, we're both going to jail."

"But the whole point was to help the dogs," she sobbed. "If we abandon them, they could get torn apart by bears or a moose. They could freeze to death or starve. They could attack somebody. They'll never get their chance."

For the first time, she realized that Matt was crying, too. Neither of them wanted this. "I wanted them to have their chance, Sofia. I did. But not at the expense of my own. Don't you understand? They could lock us up. And with my priors I wouldn't be getting out anytime soon. There's nothing left to do."

"Yes, there is." Sofia jammed down on the end call button, swallowed back the giant lump in her throat, and dialed Hunter's number.

# Thirty-Six

Although Sofia didn't say much on the phone, Hunter arrived less than half an hour after she'd placed her call for help.

"I knew you'd get in touch eventually, but I'm kind of surprised it's so soon," he said when she and Wolfie greeted him outside the apartments.

Sofia fell into his arms, finally allowing herself to sob freely in his presence. She cried for the dogs that had been burned in the fire. She cried for those she'd saved only to deliver to an uncertain future. She cried for Wolfie, and for Foxie, and for Liz. The only one she didn't cry for was herself.

She didn't deserve a single tear.

"Hey, what's wrong?" Hunter asked, clutching her tightly in his strong arms.

She took a step back and searched his eyes for the admiration she always found there. Sofia needed to remember Hunter's kind eyes before that special glint vanished forever.

His face crinkled in a smile as he reached forward and brushed the hair away from her cheeks.

"I like you so much," she whispered. "I've liked you from the beginning. But after I tell you the truth, you won't like me anymore."

"Hey, let me be the judge of that." Hunter's reassuring smile only made her fall for him harder, made her wish there had been a way for them to work out in the end. But, no, they were over before they'd even started.

"I'm going to tell you everything, but first..." She stepped forward and gently touched her lips to his. Their first kiss, their last kiss, their very best kiss. Selfish as it was, Sofia knew she couldn't go on forever without knowing what it would be like with Hunter. Without tasting love on her lips at least once.

When they pulled apart, her face was drenched with tears.

Hunter stroked her cheek with his thumb and leaned in again, but she turned away. "No," she said, her voice shaking. "Now I need tell you the truth. It's what I should have done from the beginning, but I was scared."

"Sofia, you don't have to do this. It's okay. I'm just happy that you finally called." He hugged her from behind, but Sofia pushed him off again.

"Yes, I do need to do this," she insisted, hugging her arms to her chest to keep herself from reaching back out to Hunter, from letting him distract her for even a second longer. "Can you drive us somewhere?"

He placed a hesitant hand on her shoulder. "Sure, but I don't understand."

"You will. First let's go to the textile factory you took me to on our first date, then I'll confess everything." Sofia turned to look at him one last time. When next she spoke, all the affection would drain from his hazel eyes, leaving them colorless and devoid of any love they might have eventually held for her.

But this is what her crimes had cost her. It was only fair that she be punished, deprived of what could have been...

When they pulled up to the abandoned warehouse a few brief moments later, Sofia could already hear the dogs barking from inside. Assuming she could keep them hidden here for weeks and that no one would notice was an insane fantasy. She had been so, so stupid. Confessing to Hunter was the first intelligent thing she had done for the better part of a month.

At least the ubiquitous roiling in her stomach had finally quieted, knowing relief was near at hand. Her body had always reacted so strongly to Hunter, like it knew she needed him. She'd never have guessed that it would be to mete out the justice she so badly needed—even if it would cost her everything.

"I don't have a key," he told her as they paced toward the door and the dog's barking reached a fever pitch. "But I'm guessing you know another way in."

Sofia paused and turned toward him one last time. "Just remember," she said, "I thought I was doing the right thing."

They pushed through the door and Sofia grabbed the flashlights she'd kept stashed inside. The dogs barked, howled, and whimpered as the two humans approached, spinning around in their crates like furry tops.

Hunter paused as she continued forward. It was better this way. It meant she wouldn't need to see the change in him as he slowly unrolled the truth.

"Sofia..." he asked slowly, leaving her unable to discern his mood from the softly spoken words. "Are these the dogs from the building that was burned out last night?"

Sofia bobbed her head as she filled a series of large metal bowls with kibble and handed them out to the dogs one by one. Fortunately, none of the rescues tried to leap from the cages and escape. All were just so happy to have another meal. When everyone had been fed, Sofia sank onto the dirty ground and hugged her knees to her chest.

Hunter came to sit before her so that they were face to face. "Are these the dogs from that building?" he asked again, apparently needing to hear her admission verbally before he could fully believe it.

"Yes," she said without meeting his gaze. "They were part of a dog-fighting ring and when I found out, I decided to save them."

His voice seemed far away, weakened by hurt. "Why didn't you call the cops? Why didn't you call *me*?"

"I don't know... I guess I was so blinded by my desire to help that I couldn't see any other options," she admitted, staring hard at her denim knees and trying not to wonder what Hunter must think of her now, to wonder which part of her confession would be the part where she lost his respect completely.

Hunter cleared his throat, but it still came out

strained and cracked. "Did you start the fire?" he asked.

"No! I never wanted anyone to get hurt, especially not the dogs. That's why I took them, so they would stop being hurt."

"The dogs from the fighting ring?"

She nodded and pressed her nails into her legs hard so she at least had a different type of pain to focus on for a little while. "And Foxie. And Wolfie."

The air around them thickened like a suffocating blanket of smoke.

"Foxie?" Hunter asked quietly.

"Fanta, Joe Collins's dog. I saw her in the pouring rain and thought she needed help, so I took her."

"In a red sedan." This wasn't a question, because finally Hunter knew. He knew what she'd done and hidden for what felt like an eternity.

"Yup." She forced herself to look at him now that she was free. Her part in this was over. Now it would be up to Hunter what happened next.

He frowned and kept his eyes fixed on the floor as he continued to work something out in his head. "And you took Wolfie, too?"

"He was the first one I took. He was chained to a stake all day with no food or water. It was hot, and he looked like he was suffering. I couldn't leave him there."

"Why didn't you turn yourself in after you took Wolfie? Why not end it there?" He glanced up at her but turned away the second his eyes connected with hers. Hunter couldn't even stand to look at her anymore, and she couldn't blame him. Not in the least.

She dug her nails into her legs again. Tears stained the words that followed. "Because I love him and made a promise to him. I couldn't let him get hurt again, and I couldn't lose him. But I also couldn't afford him, so a friend helped me steal supplies and then he sent his girlfriend to steal from my store, and it just became this huge vicious cycle."

"The guy with Tourette's," Hunter said with a creased brow. "The one I warned you about."

"It's not his fault. I made my own decisions."

Hunter seemed angry now that there were others who could take the blame. "Did he help you take the dogs from the fighting ring last night? Is he the one who started a fire?"

It would be so easy to say yes. She could tell Hunter wanted her to, that he wanted to fight for her, that if only someone else took the blame Sofia would still be who he'd always assumed she was. They could still have a chance.

But that wouldn't be fair to D-Man or the others. Even horrible, useless Preeti didn't deserve to be set up like this. Sofia had made the decision to confess, so she would take the full burden of responsibility. And the full punishment.

"No, I acted alone," she said with a sniff. "But I honestly don't know how the fire got started."

Both fell silent as they sat together in the near darkness. This time Sofia wasn't afraid, because the worst had already happened.

Now that her confession had been made, the only thing left was for Hunter to arrest her. So what was he waiting for?

## Thirty-Seven

S ofia couldn't stand the silence a moment longer. "Well, now you know…" she ventured, once again risking a glance at Hunter.

Hunter's face gave nothing away. He kept it flat, thoughtful, his hands folded beneath his chin. "Yes, now I know."

"So, what happens next?" *Please tell me. I can't take another second of not knowing.*

He sat up straighter and dropped his hands. "We find a place to take all these dogs."

"And then?"

Finally, an emotion showed on Hunter's handsome face, and it definitely wasn't the one Sofia expected. Not rage, not sorrow, but rather a look of tenderness overtook his expression. He smiled and said, "We finally finish our date."

"*What?* Aren't you going to arrest me?" Sofia pressed her fingernails into her legs again. This time it was to check that this was real and not some kind of crazy, demented dream.

"I could," Hunter admitted with a shrug. "I probably should, but *I won't.*"

Sofia broke down crying yet again. She felt all the things that Hunter was supposed to be feeling now. She was angry, she was hurt, but above all else, she was desperately confused.

He scooted over until they were sitting hip to hip. "My job is to uphold the law," he said softly, taking her hand in his.

She nodded, just as confused as before. "Yes, I know. That's why I thought you'd turn me in."

"My job is to uphold the law," he repeated pensively. "But you know what? There's a higher order than the laws of this city, state, or country. There's the universal law, God's law, the moral code —and according to all those, you haven't done anything wrong."

Sofia ticked off the various commandments she remembered from her days in Sunday school. "Thou shalt not steal... Thou shalt not kill... Thou shalt—"

"Thou shalt give yourself a break already. Look at you, you're shaking." Hunter put an arm around her, and she eagerly curled into his side. "I know you, Sofia, and after today, I know you even better. You're not some ruthless criminal. You're a beautiful woman with a kind heart. You wanted to save the world one dog at a time. Maybe you didn't choose the *best* methods, but how does that make what you did wrong?"

She wept into his shirt, unable to believe this was happening. That Hunter had not only justified her actions, but that he wanted to help her. "I broke the law," she argued.

"And saved how many lives?"

"The fire—"

"You said you didn't start it, and I believe you." He bent down and kissed each of her cheeks. His scratchy beard tickled, but still Sofia couldn't bring herself to laugh, to truly believe the scene that was unfolding in this desolate warehouse that held living proof of her sins.

"But how can you just forgive me after all I've done? After how much I've avoided you? Lied to you and everyone else?"

Hunter stroked her hair, his heartbeat a steady, calming presence beneath Sofia's cheek. "The same way you're eventually going to forgive yourself," he said. "You did the wrong thing for the *right* reason. As far as I'm concerned, that makes you one of the good guys. And you know what else?"

Sofia lifted her head from Hunter's chest and studied him through a curtain of unshed tears. "What?" she asked.

"If you'd never taken Wolfie, we wouldn't have met. Do you realize that?"

She smiled as Hunter pressed his lips to her forehead. "I don't know what I did to deserve you."

"It's everything you are, Sofia. It's your enormous heart. *I'm* the one who doesn't know how he got so lucky."

When he leaned forward to kiss her, Sofia didn't resist. Hunter's lips held healing, forgiveness, and maybe even love. They were exactly what she needed to finally begin to move past the guilt that had been eating her from the inside.

Hunter pulled back, but his warmth and kindness remained. "Let's get these dogs to a safe place, and then I'm going to take you on the best second half of a first date you've ever had."

Somehow, Sofia didn't doubt that.

She didn't feel guilty about it, either.

# Thirty-Eight

Sofia and Hunter returned to her apartment with a plan in place. Knowing she owed Liz a much bigger conversation, Sofia decided to instead call on her new friend, Scarlett, for help.

"Easy peezy lemon squeezy!" Scarlett cried brightly when Sofia informed her they needed a way to transport and house nine rescue dogs. Sure enough, a couple hours later, Scarlett arrived with her musher friend, Lauren, and one of the other guests Sofia recognized from the party Friday night.

"Wait a sec," Lauren said, pulling Sofia aside almost immediately after she'd entered the apartment. "Isn't this the guy I had to save you from the other night?" She hooked a thumb at Hunter, who smiled and waved.

Sofia laughed for what felt like the first time ever. "Umm, yeah."

"Well, that turned out differently than I expected." Lauren laughed, too, then slapped her hands together. "Okay, enough about that. Let's go rescue some dogs."

After everyone had been briefly reintroduced and Wolfie received a few extra reassuring pats on the head, the revamped rescue team began their mission. Sofia had no doubt things would go much better today than they had last night.

"I'll be taking the dogs back to Puffin Ridge," Lauren informed Sofia as the group descended the stairs. "It's off season, and we have the space. They'll each get their own little dog house, and we'll make sure they get plenty of exercise. First, though, Oscar here is going to check them all out and see if they need any veterinary care."

"And I'm driving," Scarlett explained as she hopped behind the wheel of the giant sled dog truck. "For old time's sake."

"Sofia," Oscar called, motioning for her to join him, "would you drive with me?"

She looked back to Hunter, who nodded and then climbed into the back of Oscar's car, leaving Sofia to ride in the front. She wasn't sure what the vet wanted, and she didn't really look forward to finding out. At least she had Hunter on her side now that she'd been brave enough to tell him the truth. She could take Oscar's wrath, disappointment, or whatever else he planned to throw her way.

Oscar turned toward her with a placating grin Sofia saw through immediately. "I don't know all the details, but you did a very good thing by saving these dogs. I'm not sure if Scarlett told you, but I run the Sled Dog Rescue Organization, and we are always looking for fosters to help take in and rehabilitate dogs."

"Thanks. I'll keep that in mind." She held tight to the chest strap on her seatbelt, waiting for the rest of what he had to say, the reason for his fake smile.

When Oscar had pulled onto the main road, he frowned and said, "Actually, there's something else I need to tell you."

Sofia waited. Prayed.

"Your dog, Wolfie. Did you get him from the same place as the others? From the fighting ring?"

Sofia felt embarrassed by her actions all over again, but she was no longer afraid, especially not with Hunter sitting behind her, offering his silent support. "No, I... *liberated*... him from a house that wasn't taking care of him."

"Ahh, that explains some things. He's an illegal wolf hybrid, you know."

"Relax, Dr. Dog," Hunter grumbled from the backseat. "*I* know about Wolfie, and I'm not turning her in. Anchorage PD, by the way."

Their driver sighed. "That's not what I'm worried about. I'm worried about Wolfie."

Sofia's breath hitched as she waited for Oscar to continue. After all this, could Wolfie still be at risk?

"I hate to be the one to tell you this, but wolf hybrids... well, they're illegal for a reason. They really shouldn't be kept as pets because they're still wild animals. They need to be free, not cooped up in some tiny apartment playing Fido."

Hunter's hand tensed on her shoulder as she struggled to make sense of what Oscar was telling her. "But Sofia loves Wolfie. She's gone out of her way to make sure he's taken care of."

"I know she has," the vet said with a sad smile. "That's why I know she'll consider what I said."

# Thirty-Nine

It took hardly any time at all for Sofia and the others to load the rescues into Lauren's sled dog truck. Oscar did a quick evaluation of each dog and chose to bring about half of them back to his clinic for further treatment.

Hunter held Sofia's hand the entire time. It meant they couldn't help as much as originally planned, but the others clearly had far more expertise than Sofia when it came to working with dogs.

"Make no mistake," Oscar reassured her when the last of the dogs were settled into the truck. "You saved their lives."

"Thank you," she mumbled, the warning he'd given her earlier that afternoon ringing in her head. She thought she'd saved Wolfie, too—but according to Oscar, he was unhappy, or at least would be someday.

"My offer stands," Oscar continued. "I'd love to have you in the SDRO's foster network. We could teach you more about rehabilitation. You could help so many dogs. Look us up online if you decide you want to go forward with it."

The three of them watched as Scarlett and Lauren backed their truck away from the warehouse and merged into the main traffic.

"Well, I have to get to the clinic, but I'll drop you off back home first," Oscar said, clutching at his keys as he strode toward his car.

"Actually, it's not too far," Sofia countered. "I think I'd like to walk."

Oscar opened the car door, but didn't get in. "You sure?" he asked with a raised eyebrow.

Sofia nodded. "Yeah, it will be good to get some fresh air into my system."

Everyone shook hands and said goodbye, then Sofia and Hunter waited for Oscar to drive away before beginning their own journey home.

"You're very brave, you know." Hunter fit his hand into hers and kissed each of her fingers.

Sofia chuckled. "You risk your life every day for work. I just sell khaki pants."

"You know your work is much bigger than that store, and it seems like you're just getting started. Are you going to take Oscar up on his offer to foster?"

She kicked at a pebble. "I don't know yet. Probably."

"What about...?" He let his words trail away and frowned.

"Wolfie," Sofia finished for him. "I don't know about that yet, either."

"You don't have to do anything you don't want to," he reminded her. "There are exceptions to every rule, and I can tell how much Wolfie loves you. He knows you saved him."

Sofia smiled thinking of how close she and her dog had become over the weeks. "I'm starting to think maybe he saved me, too."

"I don't doubt that." Hunter smiled a faraway smile as they continued down the sidewalk holding hands. "It's the same with me and Scout. Did I tell you how I got him?"

Sofia shook her head. She hadn't run into the well-mannered German Shepherd since she'd first met Hunter weeks ago. She'd have to ask Hunter over for a doggie playdate once the two humans finished their first date redo.

"I got shot..." Hunter patted his thigh as they

walked. "Right here. It wasn't even all that bad. A flesh wound, as they say. It stung for a bit, and then it didn't. But the fear stayed. Every time I got within a few miles of the place where it happened, I would tense up and have a hard time breathing. PTSD is common in the field, but I felt so stupid. I'd hardly been scratched by that bullet, and yet I couldn't stop thinking about what could have been if it had hit me just a foot or two higher. I had a *near*-near-death experience, which is nothing to write home about, except it kind of changed everything.

"I almost quit the force, but then a buddy of mine suggested I get a therapy animal. I laughed at him, of course—but when he brought Scout to my place, I was a goner. Scout's like me, you know. He trained to be a police dog, but his first real confrontation had him running and hiding. Just like the mess I'd become. It made us click. Little by little, I worked on making Scout better, and it made me better, too. Back to normal, except I had learned about the fragility of life. That there's no point in wasting time feeling scared or guilty or angry. That what ifs are for suckers. That every day was a gift."

"Wow, I had no idea," Sofia said once she was sure he'd finished his story. What she found most remarkable of all was the entire time he narrated these hard scenes from his past, Hunter wore a genuine smile. It didn't falter even once. Ever since she'd met Hunter, she'd hid from him when this whole time he was perhaps the one who could best understand her own pain, fear, and guilt.

His smile gave way to determination as he set his jaw. "That's why I wouldn't give up on you, Sofia. Even when you kept pushing me away. There was something special between us from that very first day in the vet's office, and I couldn't let that go. I had to know you, to see if we could fit just like Scout and I did."

"And?" If her cold heart hadn't already melted for Hunter, this would have turned it into a waxy puddle of goo.

Hunter held their joined hands up between them. "Looks like a perfect fit to me."

Sofia laughed and let Hunter swing her into his side and reach down to take a kiss. It was so casual, so comfortable, so perfectly them—as if they'd shared millions of kisses before and would share millions more to come. She never would have guessed the cop and robber could find true love, but it seemed they were already well on their way.

"Can I treat you to a late lunch?" Hunter asked as they strolled up to her apartment complex.

She wanted to say *yes*. Wanted to say that the answer to all future questions he planned to ask her would be yes, too. But...

"I can't," she said, standing on tiptoe to kiss him goodbye. "There's something important I need to do first."

# Forty

As she drove to Memory Ranch, Sofia thought about what she could say to convince Elizabeth Jane to forgive her. Still, she knew no amount of sorries could fix what Sofia had knowingly done to her friend. All she could really do was speak from her heart and pray that one day her friend might forgive her.

Sofia also knew that Liz could very well refuse to accept her apology altogether. And she deserved no less.

Sure enough, when Sofia knocked, Elizabeth Jane bellowed through the door, "I know why you're here, and I'm not in the mood!"

"Please," Sofia begged, but the door remained shut and Liz remained silent.

"I'll wait here all day if that's what it takes." Sofia pressed her cheek against the cool painted wood and sighed. "Please let me tell you how very sorry I am. *Please*."

When Liz still didn't respond, Sofia sank down onto the porch steps and waited. Although she had the urge to pull out her phone and get lost in a mindless little app game, she kept her hands tucked firmly under her thighs and passed the time without entertainment.

It wasn't long before Dorian joined her outside, lowering himself onto the stairs beside her. "We returned Delilah to her owner yesterday."

Suddenly, Sofia was crying... again. "I know. That must have been hard."

Dorian nodded and steepled his fingers in his lap. "It was. Especially for Liz, but the guy was really nice. He tried to give us a reward which we, of course, refused. But he also said Liz could visit Delilah—Fanta—any time, and he even told us the breeder he got her from in case we wanted to adopt a pup from a future litter."

Sofia sniffed. "This is all my fault. I'll pay for it, of course. I'll do anything to make it right. I am so, so sorry." She still didn't have any money or any prospects for money, but some way, somehow, she would figure this out for her friend.

Dorian placed a reassuring hand on her arm. "No need to do that. I'm already planning to take Liz to the next SDRO adoption event so she can pick out another new used dog. I'm not worried about that one bit. But..."

He took a deep shaky breath, and Sofia wondered if he might cry, too. "You know Liz doesn't have all that many friends. The ones she does have she trusts with her whole heart, and you broke that."

"I know. I was so selfish. I was just scared. It doesn't make it right, but—"

Dorian stopped her again. "Liz told me she shared what happened last year with her father and... well, father. That you know she's been lied to her entire life."

"Yes, I do. *I do.*" The more Dorian spoke, the worse Sofia felt. Liz was never going to forgive her, which meant Sofia would also lose her new friends, Scarlett and Lauren, in the wake of this fight.

Dorian cleared his throat, his voice remained strong and steady. "That's what makes this hurt her so deep. That someone who knew all that could still mislead her like you did."

"I was just trying to help the dog. I thought—"

"I know, and I understand. I lied to her, too, in the beginning. And I regret that every single day." Liz had forgiven Dorian, and now they were engaged to be married. But Dorian hardly knew her when he'd hurt her. Sofia had been friends with Elizabeth Jane for years, and yet that hadn't stop her from shamelessly using her friend to lessen her own guilt.

"Should I go?" Sofia asked, hating to give up but not knowing what else she could do. "I don't want to make things worse. I already hate myself for breaking her trust."

Dorian shook his head and a wistful smile crossed his face. "Like I said, she loves with her whole heart. And once you're inside, there's no getting out."

Sofia braved a smile. Could this mean it wasn't too late after all? "How can I let her know how sorry I am?"

"Show up."

"I did. I'm here," Sofia insisted, new hope swelling in her chest.

"And keep showing up." Dorian stood and brushed off the seat of his pants. "Don't give up on her, and she won't give up on you."

"So, see you again tomorrow?" Sofia ventured.

He nodded. "And the day after that."

"Could you just tell her what we talked about? Thank her for being such a good friend to me and tell her that I promise to do better. I never break my promises. Just ask Wolfie." She laughed sadly, remembering her earlier conversation with Oscar about the unknown fate of her beloved wolf hybrid.

"One day I will," Dorian said with a kind hand on Sofia's back. "We'll have you and Wolfie over to meet the new member of our pack. By then, this whole thing will be history and you and Liz will be better friends than ever."

"Do you promise?" she squeaked.

Dorian hugged her, chuckling as he did. "Yeah, and I never break a promise, either."

## Forty-One

Sofia left the ranch, but not before handwriting an apology letter to her poor friend Elizabeth Jane. Dorian promised to pass the note on to his fiancée and told Sofia he would also have a talk with Liz on her behalf.

When Sofia made it back to her apartment, she was surprised to find Hunter waiting on the stoop outside her building.

"What are you doing here?" she asked, falling into his arms with a grateful sigh.

"Well, it's about a quarter past 6:30." He flashed his phone before her eyes to prove his point. "You said we could have a second chance at our first date, and last time I picked you up at 6:30. So here I am again."

Sofia chuckled and stretched to kiss him on the cheek. Funny how natural it felt now when their first kiss had only happened earlier that day.

A dark thought made her fall silent again. "I don't want to go back to the textile factory." Hunter had given her a special place, and she'd wasted no time in tainting it with bad memories. Now she couldn't think of the building without also remembering the horrible stench of the fighting ring and the fire that followed.

Hunter hummed in agreement. "Understood. I actually found a different place to take you this time, but first, can we have some dinner? I'm starved."

"*Mmm*, me too. Are we going to the Conoco-Phillips like you had planned before?" *Food*. She hadn't eaten anything the whole day, as her stomach now reminded her with a rolling groan.

They both laughed and kissed again.

"Not this time," Hunter said. "Couldn't book it on such short notice, but I did have time to make some home-cooked vegan fare for the two of us to share in the park."

Sofia pulled back to stare at him with wide, horrified eyes. "Wait, you're a vegan?"

Hunter looked equally shocked as he insisted, "No, I thought you were."

"*Eww*, why?" She smushed her face into a grimace.

"All the selfless animal love?"

They both broke apart in giggles and kissed again.

"Just goes to show how much we still have to learn about each other."

"Well, usually we'd get these things out of the way on our first date, which is why we have to try to get it right this time." Hunter winked at her, causing Sofia to laugh again.

"Hey, I'm ready, if you are."

"Me, too." He held his hand out, which Sofia gladly clasped between her own as they headed forth together.

Despite the startling lack of any dairy or meat, Hunter's picnic meal turned out to be fully edible, and maybe even a little bit delicious though neither would admit it.

"Next time I'm taking you to a steak house," Hunter promised while gnawing on some kind of seaweed wrapped morsel. When night began to fall, he draped an arm over Sofia's shoulder and pulled her closer to his side. "Ready for part two?"

Sofia stretched up to kiss him. "And three." Then kissed him again. "And four."

"And five?" Hunter asked, initiating yet another kiss. "But we seriously have to stop there or you won't get your surprise."

They both laughed as they belted into his truck. Sofia's heart skipped a beat when he delivered them both to the police station.

"Don't look so nervous," Hunter said, kissing her hand. "I promise you'll like it." He guided her inside, said a few quick hellos, and then led her to the roof.

"What is it with you and roofs?" Sofia asked with a giggle, still breathing heavily from the anxiety of walking through the station. *Stop thinking of yourself as a criminal. You're on the straight and narrow now.*

Hunter stretched his arms high overhead, then did some kind of *Karate Kid* move that had Sofia bursting with laughter. "Like you, I enjoy being one with nature."

"Are you sure you're not the vegan?" she asked between gasps for air. "Because if so, you should probably just admit it now. I'm pretty sure I'll like you anyway."

"Wow, you would like me even then?" he asked with a wink as he rummaged in a metal box pressed against the door wall.

"Even then," she assured him.

"Jeez, it's like we're already halfway to happily ever after."

Sofia giggled. "Well, it's only our second first date, so I guess we'll have to wait and see."

"Speaking of seeing things, check this out." He pulled an old projector from the box and blew a thin layer of dust off the case.

"Are you going to show me slides from your vacation?" she joked. Each moment she spent with him felt lighter and lighter, easier and easier, like it was meant to be.

"Nope, even better. Hold this." Hunter gently handed her the projector, then pulled a pair of bean bag chairs out from behind a potted plant.

Sofia laughed so hard she almost dropped her parcel.

"Careful now," he warned. "That's vintage 1990's."

"Well, there's a decade I never want to see again." Images Sofia hated remembering flashed across her mind. Celeste and Allie laughing, taunting. Sofia crying, plotting her revenge, and...

"I bet you were hot back then, too." Hunter kissed her on the cheek and took the projector back from her hands. "Okay, pick your favorite bean bag chair and point it at—" He motioned toward a gray facade of bricks across the roof. "—That wall."

Sofia shook her head to clear out the last of the high school memories. "What is it?"

He glanced up from the rickety side table on which he was arranging the projector. "That? It's a storage shed."

"No, your plan. What are we doing?" She hit him playfully in the shoulder and he grabbed her wrist, pulling her into his chest.

"Drive-in theater, no car required," he said with a proud grin.

"I've never been to a drive-in before."

Hunter kissed the top of her head, then released her from his arms. "You're going to love it, especially when you see what we're watching."

"Ooh, what?" Hunter was an expert at building the anticipation. Sofia had never like surprises before, but maybe with him she could learn. Especially if he kept up this cute, haughty act whenever he had something special to reveal.

True to form, Hunter wagged a finger at her. "Nope, you'll have to wait and see like the rest of the audience."

Sofia laughed yet again. "Well, I'm assuming *you* already know, seeing as you set this whole thing up."

"But that sparrow over there—" He pointed again where, sure enough, a little bird sat fluffing its feathers. "He's excited for the surprise. Now take a seat, and let the show begin."

Sofia carefully arranged herself in the bean bag chair, letting the tiny Styrofoam beads cradle her rump in a way that fell just short of heaven.

Hunter dragged his bag closer so the two of them could hold hands as the opening credits streamed through the projector in a single bright beam. When the old Universal Studios logo spun its way across the globe with an exciting string crescendo, Sofia squealed and clapped her hands.

"Yup, definitely a child of the nineties," Hunter observed with a laugh. "But it's okay, because I am, too. Oh, hey. Catch!" He leaned forward and dragged the metal box closer, then tossed two shiny snack packages her way.

Sofia studied them in her hands, a rush of nostalgia warming her heart. "A Fruit Roll-Up and... Capri Sun?"

"Yeah, they're vegan, right?" Hunter joked, then seeing the look on Sofia's face added, "Next time I'll make sure to get Combos and Nesquik since I know you can handle the real stuff."

They each punched the little yellow straws into their silver drink pouches, then did a cheers.

"You know," Sofia said after a long, luxurious sip, "I'm starting to think that maybe not everything about growing up is so bad after all."

"It got you here," Hunter pointed out, balling up the Fruit Roll-Up and shoving the whole thing in his mouth.

"It got me here. And..." She turned her attention back to the movie where a cartoon dog ran across the screen. "Wait, is this... Is this *Balto*? This movie's almost as old as I am!"

"I figured you would like it. After all, my man Balto's half dog, half wolf. Plus, he saves the day. Kind of like you and Wolfie."

"So I'm half dog?" Sofia asked, faking an outraged expression.

"Hey, I didn't mean it like that. Wolfie's the half-breed, and you're the hero."

A hero. She liked that.

And she liked this.

To think she had almost thrown it all away.

# Forty-Two

The next day, Sofia returned to work a new woman. So much had happened over the weekend to forever change her life, and she planned to continue on the road to redemption until she'd finally rid herself of every last ounce of guilt.

Following up on their call, the owner, Jean, had set aside security footage for her to review during her downtime, but Sofia already planned to confess for her part in Preeti's thefts.

If she lost her job, then so be it. But Jean deserved to know.

The best way to cure a guilty conscience, she'd begun to discover, was to show your full hand and let the cards fall where they may. No more hiding, cheating, or lying. No more bending the rules and squeezing through to get what she wanted.

It was time to live an honest life—to completely commit.

And, sure enough, despite Sofia's attempts to block the cameras at the time, the tape had clearly picked up Preeti's shoplifting and the fact that Sofia had watched the whole time from less than three feet away. The tapes also revealed that when Sofia had gone to the back of the store to retrieve a different-sized garment for a customer, Preeti had deftly unlocked the cash register and grabbed a wad of twenties. Sofia felt so betrayed. She hadn't even noticed her keycard missing at the time.

Of course, she'd tell Jean everything—that she'd rescued Wolfie from that dumpy yard, that a friend had stolen the pet supplies she couldn't afford, and then in turn blackmailed her in order to steal from Jean's store. She would take full responsibility, but there was no hiding Preeti's face from the security footage. There weren't many Indian people in Alaska, and even fewer who hung around the mall during the work day. Preeti would be identified within hours, if not faster.

Sofia's skin still prickled whenever she thought of

Preeti—how the girl had forced them to involve her in the rescue, then refused to help and accidentally started a fire when they were making their escape. Getting nailed for shoplifting and petty theft would be a far lighter sentence than she actually deserved. It wasn't up to Sofia to decide but she could at least offer Preeti a heads up about what would soon be coming her way.

Unable to look upon the girl who had caused her so many problems, Sofia instead decided to text Blinky: *Come by at lunch. There's something you need to know.*

"Sofi, you have the D-Man all kinds of worked up," Blinky announced, striding into her store an hour later. "What did you do to him?"

Sofia groaned. She was not in the mood for this happy banter, not when people and animals had been seriously hurt. "I'm sure Preeti's already told you everything, so cut the act."

"Yikes. Not your best self today, eh?"

She scowled at him. Was this really all a big joke to Blinky? To the others? "Don't you feel bad about... everything that happened?"

He shrugged, but then his head jerked to the side and a twitching fit took him over. "Things happen, especially when you're not careful. Next time he'll be more careful."

"Maybe he will," Sofia answered thoughtfully. "But there's not going to be a next time for me. And there might not be for your girlfriend either."

"Whoa, hey now!" Blinky closed the distance between them and leaned over her counter, bringing his voice to barely above a whisper. "What's that supposed to mean?"

"It means," Sofia gestured toward the monitor she'd been using to review the store's video feed. "Our security cams caught her stealing the other day, and my boss is going to see this when she comes in later tonight."

"Is that all?" Blinky laughed, but his facial convulsions gave away his underlying anxiety. "Destroy the tapes. Problem solved."

She crossed her arms over her chest and stared him down. "No, I can't do that."

"Are you serious, Sofi? Don't be ridiculous. If you don't destroy the tapes, then you'll be caught, too. I know you stood by and watched. The camera must have picked you up, too."

"It did." He had her there, but what he didn't know is how little she cared about getting caught herself. She just wanted to make things right for Jean and everyone else.

"Then what are you going to do?" He laughed again. It's what he always did, whether happy, sad, cruel, scared. She wouldn't miss his laugh when it was gone. "Make creative edits to the video because you have some kind of grudge against my girl?"

Sofia sighed. "No, I'm going to turn the tapes in as-is. I never wanted any of this. I'm done."

Blinky shook his head and continued to laugh bitterly. "You think I dragged you in kicking and screaming? *No.* You asked for my help, and I gave it to you. You can't have it both ways, darlin."

"I know that now," she said softly.

"So you don't want to be my friend anymore? *Boo hoo.* Give me the footage and I'll leave you alone, princess, but I'm not leaving here without it."

"Then I guess you'll be here when my boss arrives. That will be awkward."

Blinky raised back to his full height. His brows pinched in anger, but his voice remained steady. "I don't get what your deal is today, but let me remind you we can make your life very hard. You've done a lot worse than shoplifting. What if we turned you into your cop boyfriend? I bet he'd love to slap some cuffs on you."

Blinky stared at her, but she refused to budge. Sofia was done being pushed around. She was done hurting others and done letting them hurt her. "If that's what you think, Matt, then you've never been my friend. Now get out of my store."

# Forty-Three

A couple days later, D-Man showed up outside Sofia's door. While he'd never been to her apartment, he had briefly visited the building when he returned her car that fateful Saturday night. Sofia hadn't heard from Blinky or any of his friends since Preeti's arrest on Monday, but she'd always known that if anyone was going to reach out to her, it would be D-Man. Now that he was here, however, she had no idea what to expect.

"Going to yell at me?" she asked, placing a hand on each hip as she strode the rest of the way up the sidewalk.

"Are you going to yell at me?" he countered after rising to his feet.

She offered him a hesitant smile. "No," she said, drawing out the word.

D-Man blushed and hung his head. "Then I won't either."

"What are you doing here, Matt?" she asked, cutting to the chase since it seemed her visitor was having a hard time bringing them there. "I already turned Preeti in, so it's too late to change my mind."

He shook his head adamantly. "*Change your mind?* No, I wanted to thank you."

This was definitely not what Sofia had expected. "Thank me?"

"Yes, *thank you*. I never said it before for you helping with the rescue, so *thank you*. I also want to say it now, because..." His entire head turned red with embarrassment again. "Well, you inspire me."

"Umm, you're going to have to explain that one." She sunk to the doorstep, not ready to invite Matt into her apartment but also not strong enough to stand at the moment.

D-Man sat down beside her even though he'd only just stood up moments before. "You were so brave," he gushed with the largest smile she'd ever seen him wear. "Turning yourself and Preeti in like that. In making sure the dogs were taken care of when I wanted to dump them in a field just to make my own problems go away. I wish I could have had the courage to follow through and help those dogs, but when I ran away scared, you're the one who stepped up."

Sofia rubbed him on the shoulder. It was nice to hear she'd done something good after all. She studied the full sleeve of tattoos on Matt's left arm as they spoke. One of them looked raw and new, covering his wrist and part of the back of his hand. It looked like a cocktail of some kind, perhaps a Shirley Temple.

"Do you know what it's like to constantly have to look back over your shoulder, waiting to be caught, waiting to be found out?" Matt continued, smiling when he caught her examining his newest ink.

"Yeah, I think I might know something about that," she admitted with a laugh. "I like your tattoo."

"Which one?" He laughed and held up his hand. "I'm guessing the newest, yeah? Did it myself last night, actually. Like I said, you inspire me, and now I always have a little reminder of that inspiration with me."

"I don't drink," Sofia reminded him.

"And now, neither do I." D-Man's eyes danced

with unshed tears. This wasn't the look of sadness, but rather strength.

"What? You're going sober? Really?" Sofia hadn't known D-Man for long, but they had been through so much together already. The fact that he credited her for any part of this monumental decision made her want to cry big, happy tears.

"Yup. No time like the present. And yes, I'm not just getting sober. I'm getting clean. I'm following your lead. You cut ties with Blinky and the others, and I'm going to as well. And I'm going to stop selling and get myself an honest job."

Sofia gave Matt a long hug. "I'm so glad to hear that. I guess you won't be going by D-Man any more, huh?"

He laughed and shook his head. "Nope, it's just Matt now."

"I like that much better anyway," she said with a wink.

"Me too."

They watched a flock of birds fight over an unseen food source in the courtyard. Sofia had once been like those birds, fighting so hard for so little. But now she didn't need to anymore, because she'd remembered that she could fly--and now Matt could, too.

"The other reason I'm here is because, this is going to sound so lame," Matt continued when the last of the birds had fled. "But I wanted to ask if we could still be friends. Now that I'm going down the straight and narrow, I could really use a friend at my side. And if you say yes, you'll be the only one I've got now."

"I'm guessing Blinky wasn't happy to hear about any of this," Sofia said, remembering her final confrontation with the other Matt as well.

Her friend laughed. "Let's just say he had a lot of choice words about how the two of us deserve each other."

"You know what? I think he's right." She patted him on the shoulder and pulled herself back to her feet. "I'd love to be your friend, D-Ma—I mean, Matt. C'mon up and I'll make you some dinner. Although I've gotta warn you, I'm not a very good cook."

Matt stood, too, but did not look pleased about the invitation. "That might be a little difficult," he said. "Umm, I'm a vegan."

Sofia burst out laughing so hard, she had to struggle for breath.

"I'm serious," Matt said, joining her in a laugh anyway. "I really am vegan."

"A vegan drug dealer? Now I've heard of everything."

"A vegan *ex* drug dealer, thank you very much," he reminded her.

"Matt," Sofia said, slinging an arm over his shoulder as they headed inside. "You're definitely one in a million, and I'm so glad we're friends."

# Forty-Four

Growing up, Sofia had always liked her father best when he was actively attending his Alcoholics Anonymous meetings. No, he'd never hurt her or her mother—at least not physically—but he'd been enough of a wreck to make Sofia swear off alcohol for life before she'd ever even tasted a drop.

When he was in the program, though, he came home happy. He apologized to Sofia and her mother for all the various ways he'd hurt them, and he'd shown them all the true self that had been drowning from the never-ending downpour of scotch and whiskey.

Sofia wasn't an addict, but she'd learned the twelve-step recovery program long ago and knew now that she needed to make direct amends to those she had hurt. Besides Liz, there were two very notable people who still needed to know how she'd wronged them and how very sorry she was for it.

Liz wasn't ready yet to see Sofia face-to-face, but the two had started texting again. Elizabeth Jane had even invited Sofia to the welcome home party she was planning once she'd finalized the adoption for her new dog, the same young Pitbull Sofia had personally delivered from the fighting ring. She and Dorian planned to name him Rigby after some book they'd read together earlier that year. The coming home party was still another week away, but Sofia looked forward to finally being able to apologize in person.

Meanwhile, she knew her new friend, Scarlett, would be happy to help. And sure enough, she arranged everything for Sofia's final apology, including lending her own apartment as the meeting place.

"I think you're very brave," Scarlett said when Sofia revealed her plan. "I hope they'll forgive you. I know I would!"

Celeste arrived first, and then Allie about ten minutes later. Both wore matching expressions of confusion as they waited for Sofia to reveal why she'd asked them there.

"Thank you for coming," Sofia said after Scarlett had provided everyone with sweet tea and snacks. "I asked you here today so I could apologize face-to-face."

"Apologize?" Celeste snorted. "We were the ones who were awful to you. I'm honestly surprised you're even talking to us. *I'm* sorry, and I'm sure Allie is, too."

Allie shrugged, but remained silent.

Sofia smiled and reminded herself that she was here to focus on what *she'd* done, not to rehash all the reasons why. "Yeah, you did kind of make my school years hell," she told them casually. "But it doesn't excuse what I did."

Both former classmates watched her with wide eyes.

Scarlett nodded for Sofia to go ahead.

"I was so angry back then," she continued. "I wanted to make you suffer the way you did to me. So I planned a prank."

"The graffiti! *You* did it?" Allie shifted her gaze toward Celeste, seeming far angrier at her than at Sofia. "I told you it wasn't me, but you wouldn't even believe your best friend when she told you she was innocent."

Celeste frowned. "I don't understand. Why did you frame Allie? Why not me?"

"I framed you both in a way. I knew you would fight and both get into trouble. I was counting on the two of you getting expelled, and knew I had to go big to make that happen. So I trashed the gym and spray-painted Celeste is a... well, *you know*... over every inch of those walls. I stole your notebook from English class, Allie, and studied the handwriting so it would match. I am so sorry for what I did." Sofia hung her head and waited for her two former bullies to tear into her.

Celeste remained quiet, thoughtful, but Allie grew noticeably angry.

"Well, it worked like a charm, didn't it?" she cried. "And to think I felt guilty all these years!"

"I felt terrible when I found out what happened," Sofia said, fighting back tears. "I just wanted you to leave me alone. I didn't mean to ruin your life."

"Ruin my life?" Allie asked, her brows pinching together in confusion. "Are you talking about Millie?"

Sofia nodded. "If you hadn't been forced to go to

that new school, you never would have met that boy, you never would have gotten pregnant. You could have had the life you wanted, but I took that away from you."

"Sofia, *no*," Allie said with a grave look on her face. "Yes, what you did sucks, but you didn't end my life. You gave it to me. Millie is my everything. I can't picture a world without her in it. So, I guess, thank you, actually. Everything turned out okay in the end."

"You're not mad?" Sofia looked from Allie to Celeste, both of whom wore sad smiles.

"Believe me, I would have been furious back then, but we're all pushing thirty here now. We're not little kids. Celeste and I honestly deserved it—far worse, probably. If anyone ever tries to pick on Millie, I'd be doing a lot worse to them." Allie laughed, and it sucked all the tension from the air.

"I told you it would be okay!" Scarlett said, refilling everyone's glasses.

"But what I don't get," Celeste said, chewing on a hangnail. "Is why would you want to confess now? What difference does it make?"

Sofia thought about that for a moment. In a way, she was just ticking off the boxes for her own twelve-step recovery program—but that wasn't the answer she would give. "It's hard to move forward when you're anchored to your past mistakes. I guess I was just finally ready to move forward. To be free," she admitted.

Celeste smiled and clinked her tea against Sofia's and then Allie's. "I like that. I think I'll move forward with you. Can you forgive me for the brat I was back then? I've always felt so guilty for picking on you."

"I never would have guessed that Celeste was a bully," Scarlett said. "She's always super nice whenever I run into her in the halls."

"Thanks," Celeste said.

"Yes, forgiveness all around," Sofia said.

"And me too," Allie said. "No more anchors for any of us."

They spent the rest of the evening sharing stories of their adult lives. Both Allie and Celeste had grown up into strong, kind women with passions of their own. Sofia even enjoyed spending time with them, which would have shocked her younger self to no end. By the end of their time together, she had no problem asking for the special favor she needed.

# Forty-Five

***Five months later***

S ofia's boots crunched as she navigated the
icy trail. She hurried as fast as she could
without risking a slip and spill into the giant
mounds of snow. Oh, she had so much news to share
today!

Reaching the peak enclosure, she fell to her
haunches and called, "Wolfie! Wolfie!"

A giant gray streak of fur that was half wolf, half
dog came bounding over to the fence, licking Sofia's
fingers eagerly. When Wolfie had first been rehomed
at the Eagle River Wolf Sanctuary, Sofia had struggled to bring herself to visit. Every time she saw him,
she was reminded of how he had enriched her life

and how much she missed him now that he was gone.

But soon, something wonderful happened. A new rescue dog named Ravenna was brought to the sanctuary, and Sofia's dear, sweet Wolfie found love. Sure enough, the hulking German Shepherd wolf hybrid came bounding over to say hello to Sofia now.

"Hey, you two!" Sofia said with a giggle. "You'll never believe what happened this week!"

Wolfie sat and waited, his amber eyes boring into hers.

"Well, first off, Crash, the Newfoundland dog I told you about, he got adopted! His new owners are in love with him, slime and all. I told Oscar that he could bring a new foster by this weekend. I love seeing my doggies find their own happily ever afters!"

Ravenna barked. She, too, loved Sofia's stories.

"Okay, so the other awesome thing that happened is Lolly wore the dress I designed for her for this interview on *the Late Show*, and, well... orders are through the roof! I made more than five thousand dollars while I was sleeping last night. Can you believe it?"

It was true. Once Sofia had made all her apologies and life had begun to return to normal, she took Scarlett's advice and found a way to work animal inspiration into her line. She'd worn her first Wolfie-inspired gown to a fundraiser for the Sled Dog Rescue Organization later that month, and Oscar's wife, the country music star, Lolly Winston, had asked if Sofia could make her one, too.

The rest, as they say, was history.

They were even planning a photo shoot at the wolf sanctuary with various local celebrities posing in dresses custom designed by Sofia. Her enemy-turned-friend Celeste Lyons was hired to take the photos. And of course, the sanctuary's head tour guide, Allie Mayfair, had organized the entire thing.

Sofia still couldn't believe how full her life had become these last few months, and all because she'd loved a dog.

"Hey, sorry I'm late!" Hunter waved from the bottom of the hill, then jogged the rest of the way up the trail. When he reached the top, he scooped Sofia into a hug and gave her a kiss hello. "How's our favorite hybrid couple today?"

"Happy and in love," Sofia replied, rubbing her nose against Hunter's.

"Aww, just like us!" he teased, giving her a longer, fuller kiss.

"Dork," Sofia said, reaching for the zipper on

Hunter's coat and pulling it down. "No more stalling. I want to see it!"

"But it's cold," Hunter continued to poke fun at her, but when Sofia stamped her foot, he took off his winter coat to reveal his new tattoo. "What do you think, bud?" Hunter asked, bending down to show Wolfie the stunning likeness inked onto his bicep.

Sofia gasped. "It looks just like him. I love it! Now I want one, too."

"Well, call Matt and make an appointment then. You know he's very busy these days."

Sofia did know, and she was so proud of her friend for following his passions and becoming one of the most requested tattoo artists in Anchorage despite being so new to the scene.

"I was thinking," Hunter said, shrugging back into his coat. "That you should get Ravenna. You know, then we'd have a matching set. A couple's tattoo."

"I like how you think," Sofia said with a smile.

"And you know what else we could have matching?" Hunter asked with a huge grin stretched across his adorable, scruffy face.

Sofia thought, but came up blank. "Tell me!"

"So impatient," Hunter tsked. "That's why I knew I couldn't wait another second longer. Otherwise you'd read me the riot act. Okay, check these out." Hunter reached into his pants pocket and pulled out a little velvet box.

"Is that...?"

"I'll get straight to the point," Hunter said, clearing his throat before he continued. "Sofia Stepanov, you have the right to a happily ever after. Anything you wish can and will be granted. You have the right to a husband who loves you. If you do not already have a husband, one shall be granted to you via the acceptance of this proposal. Do you understand what I'm asking you now? And with all this in mind, do you agree to marry me?"

"Hunter Burke, you are the biggest dork in the whole wide world," Sofia said with a grin she just couldn't contain. "And I can't wait for you to be my husband."

**Ready for more heartfelt and heartwarming stories? Then make sure you're on Melissa's list so that you hear about all her new releases, special giveaways, and other sweet bonuses.**

**You can do that here: <u>MelStorm.com/gift</u>**

# More Melissa

*New York Times* and *USA Today* bestselling author Melissa Storm is happiest with a book in her hands and a pet on her lap.

Her most exciting adventures have always been born of her own "overactive imagination," a burden which often got her into trouble as a child. Now that she's grown, however, she receives accolades for her inventive tales of romance, humor, sweetness, and inspiration.

This shy, indoorsy authoress lives in the heart of Alaska with her husband, her daughter, and a lively domestic zoo brimming with spoiled cats and dogs.

Melissa dreams of one day raising bees in her back-yard, but has promised her daughter that she will resist this particular temptation. For now.

Be sure to sign up for her newsletter at **www. MelStorm.com**.

## ALSO BY MELISSA STORM

Learn more about Melissa's collected works, so that you can decide which book you'd like to read next...

## ALASKAN HEARTS

Get ready to fall in love with a special pack of working and retired sled dogs, each of whom change their new owners' lives for the better, and a sprawling ranch located just outside Anchorage helps its patients regain their lives, love, and futures.

**Start with book 1, The Loneliest Cottage.**

## ALASKA SUNRISE ROMANCES

Brothers, sisters, cousins, and friends—are all about to learn that love has a way of finding you when you least expect it. These books are short, sweet, and sure to put a smile on your face!

**Start with book 1, Must Love Music.**

## THE SUNDAY POTLUCK CLUB

This group of friends met in the cancer ward of the local hospital. They've been there for each other through the hard times. Now it's time to heal...

**Start with book 1, The Sunday Potluck Club.**

## FIRST STREET CHURCH ROMANCES

Sweet and wholesome small town love stories with the community church at their center make for the perfect feel-good reads.

**Start with book 1, Love's Prayer.**

## CHARLESTON HEARTS

A very special litter of Chihuahua puppies born on Christmas day is adopted by the local church and immediately set to work as tiny therapy dogs.

**Start with book 1, A New Life.**

## STAND-ALONE NOVELS

**The Letter from Eleanor**: From a patient's dying wish to a whirlwind of secrets, Sarah and Finch discover love amidst a legacy of intrigue.

**A Colorful Life**: Three women, three stories, one vibrant tapestry of life, love, and rediscovery.

**A Mother's Love**: In the realm of angels, one mother's undying love battles fate to reunite with her child.

**A Girl's Best Friend**: When a rising plus-size fashion star meets a playboy fitness heir, they'll have to decide whether love is really only skin-deep.

**Love & War**: War separated them, life reshaped them, but the heart's call echoes through the years.

# What to Read Next!

When Sarah Campbell agrees to help her dying patient "set things right," she never anticipated that such a simple request would completely upend her quiet life.

Enter Finch Jameson, the genius behind a global social network. Though usually shrouded in solitude, he can't ignore the secrets Eleanor's letter hides.

Together, they're plunged into a decades-old cold case, one intertwining their lives in unforeseen ways. And as each new clue is uncovered, they find themselves drawing closer to the truth--and also to each other.

But as secrets from the past and present collide, will Sarah and Finch's budding relationship prove strong enough to withstand the storm of Eleanor's legacy?

**The Letter from Eleanor is now available.**

**CLICK HERE to get your copy so that you can start reading today!**

# Sneak Peek

## THE LETTER FROM ELEANOR

Sarah let go of her patient's hand and watched as it settled back on the rumpled hospital blanket. Just yesterday Mr. Hinkley had regaled her with stories of his youthful heroics, of his time spent serving their country in Korea, and of the big, loving family that came after.

For more than eighty years he'd lived life as best as he could figure out how... and now?

He'd died alone in a nursing home, attended only by a nurse and her faithful therapy dog.

Her Golden Retriever whined and nudged the old man's hand one final time before looking to Sarah for guidance.

"Good job, Lucky," she whispered to the dog while pulling herself slowly to her feet. Sometimes she cried when residents left them. Other days she just felt numb. Whatever the particular case, saying that final goodbye never got any easier.

Not for Sarah, and certainly not for Lucky.

"Let's go for a walk," she told the dog as they click-clacked down the hall.

Lucky wagged his tail weakly. They both needed the warm California sun on their faces to coax the life back into them. It was part of their routine—treat, comfort, move on. If they mourned too long, then they wouldn't be on their best game for the other patients who needed them.

And so many needed them.

Each new person who passed through this facility offered Sarah a new life to try on, a new person to become. Outside of her work, her life had been rather unremarkable. She'd always done what was expected when it was expected. She'd gone to school, received straight A's, stayed out of trouble, and treated others with as much kindness as she could muster. Sarah was a good person, but not the kind anyone would remember when she herself passed.

She'd been working at the Redwood Cove Rest Home for the past four years now, and more than three of them with Lucky at her side. Of course,

Sarah hadn't originally planned to turn her pet into a colleague, but now she couldn't imagine herself getting through the day without the big yellow fur ball with her every step of the way.

When she'd first approached Carol Graves about adopting one of her famous Golden Retriever puppies, Sarah had only wanted a companion. Once she had secured a degree, a job, and a home, adding a dog to the mix seemed the natural next step. And because Sarah always did her best in all things, she naturally chose the most respected breeder in the entire state.

Carol Graves only bred one litter per year—and only Golden Retrievers. She'd devoted her life to the breed when one such dog had saved her from drowning as a little girl decades before Sarah had even been born.

Most of Carol's dogs went on to work in service, rescue, or even entertainment. In fact, when Sarah had first met the wriggling litter of two-month-old pups, she'd been immediately drawn to a frisky little female who was later named Star. Star now served as a co-host for the local cable morning show. Both Sarah and Lucky enjoyed watching her each day as they ate their breakfast.

But while Sarah had been drawn to Star, Lucky

only had eyes for Sarah. Of course, the erstwhile breeder insisted the two were meant to belong to each other—and that was that. Lucky actually came with his name, too. Carol had named him on the day after he was born. She hadn't expected the tiny runt of the litter to survive the night, but he'd surprised her and earned his name in the process.

Lucky had grown into a big, strong adult. No one would ever have guessed he nearly died the same day he was born. Maybe it was that near brush that made him so good with the hospice patients now. He'd been where they were going. He understood and wanted to help.

Which he did. Sometimes Sarah felt as if Lucky was the real medical wonder and that she was merely his assistant.

The Golden Retriever had a knack for knowing which residents were nearing the end, and he made sure they were never without cuddles in their final days. Once they passed on, he switched his attention to Sarah, who felt each loss deeply, no matter how hard she tried to toughen up.

Each death meant losing a patient, a friend, and a life she had tried on while enjoying all the stories and memories—temporarily adopting them as her own.

It was easier that way. Easier than finding her own life and making sure she lived it perfectly.

Just as the breeder Carol Graves had chosen her profession to celebrate a life saved, Sarah Campbell became a hospice nurse to honor the life she'd failed to rescue.

It had been her job to keep her grandmother company that summer day, to help her with anything she needed, and to keep her safe. Sarah had only been fourteen then—far more interested in talking with the attractive twin guys next door than in hearing another of her grandma's rambling stories for the millionth time.

Sarah's selfishness had meant she wasn't there when her grandmother needed help remembering whether she had taken her medication or not. In search of her wayward granddaughter, she'd slipped out of the house and down the front stairs. The ice-slicked steps led to a terrible fall she was just too weak to recover from.

Sarah still remembered the scream. It hadn't been loud and earth-shattering like you'd imagine, but rather meek—a tiny bird letting out a small, shaky chirp as it fell from its nest and crashed to the ground below.

That was the end of one life for Sarah and the

start of many others. Yet no matter how many she helped in their final days, she could never quite find a way to forgive herself for letting her grandmother down, for killing the old woman she'd loved with her negligence. Even moving clear across the country, to a place where the winter months remained bright and sunny, hadn't alleviated her guilt. The only relief she had was in doing her best, giving her full attention to those who were left.

Just as she and Lucky had done for poor Mr. Hinkley. They'd done everything by the book. And still... still, she couldn't shake the enormous feeling of disappointment.

As she passed through the automatic doors and headed outside into the facility gardens, Sarah wondered if she would ever have great stories of her own to tell, if her life would ever become more than a vehicle for her heavy guilt, if a change was coming... and if she would welcome it when it arrived.

Finch Jameson had nothing left—no family, no job prospects, and not too much money, either.

Had it really only been five years since he'd been

named one of the top thirty business tycoons under thirty?

Yes—five *long* years.

He'd made that list exactly one time before he bought into his own hype and ruined everything. Now, instead of being among the top thirty brightest young minds in the country, he'd become the number one failure, the poster boy for wasted potential.

Growing up, all he had wanted was to take beautiful pictures with his endless parade of yellow disposable cameras. He'd once aspired to be a nature photographer—to see his name in big bold letters plastered across *National Geographic* magazine. Once he hit his teen years, his passion shifted to fashion photography and all the gorgeous models such a career path would bring trotting through his bedroom.

Then, in his second year of college, a stroke of genius took hold of him and refused to let go. With a huge vision and an even more massive team of helpers, Finch brought his big idea to life.

*Reel Life.*

His fledgling social media network quickly overtook the flashing gifs of MySpace to become the go to place for people to share their lives with the world.

Reel Life Finch watched as MySpace Tom sold big and went on to enjoy a relatively anonymous and carefree life.

And he wanted that for himself.

He'd had his time in the spotlight and was ready to travel the world, taking pictures and enjoying every single moment of every day.

He eagerly agreed to sell Reel Life to the first person who asked.

As it turned out, he sold far too soon and for far too little. Seemingly overnight he went from "the one to watch" to the laughingstock of the free world. Luckily, neither of his parents had lived long enough to see his fall from grace. Still, Finch could have benefited from their love and support at the time when all the rest of his friends—and girlfriends—had abandoned him.

With nothing left, he abandoned LA to settle in the small coastal town of Redwood Cove. The money went fast, mostly due to a string of poor investments and bad advice.

"Why don't you just come up with another idea?" everyone asked.

But Finch was fresh out of brilliant inventions. Reel Life had been the pinnacle, and now at thirty-one years old, his life was already on the decline. His blazing passion for photography dulled to the tiniest of sparks buried within a giant mountain of dying embers.

It was all just too painful, too much of a reminder of what he'd not only lost but willingly given away.

Somewhere in the midst of yet another day whittling away at the time between waking up and going back to sleep, a letter arrived.

Not an email, but an old-fashion letter scrawled carefully in large looping cursive.

*Dear Finch,* it read, *I'm your great aunt Eleanor, and I'm dying. There's something very important I need to tell you before I go. Please come see me at the Redwood Cove Rest Home. I pray this letter finds you well... and before it's too late to set things right.*

*Regards,*
*Eleanor Barton*

Finch read the letter three times over before folding it back up and slipping it into the torn envelope. A great aunt? No, that was impossible. His mother loved celebrating what little family they had.

She wouldn't have let them grow estranged from one of the few surviving relatives.

He'd never once heard of the Bartons. Why would this sickly old woman reach out to him? How could she have gotten her wires so badly crossed? Made such a huge mistake?

He had half a mind to crumple the letter and toss it in the trash. This clearly wasn't his problem. But then again...

His imagination conjured a withered old waif of a woman staring forlornly out the window waiting for her lost nephew to return to her side. Could he really let her die thinking her attempt to mend fences had been met with cold refusal?

He didn't owe this woman anything, but he also couldn't live with yet another burden on his conscience. It was bad enough he'd tossed his own life in the crapper. The least he could do is help this sweet old lady find her family.

One good deed for the day, then he could return to his lackluster life.

**The Letter from Eleanor is now available.**

**CLICK HERE to get your copy so that you can start reading today!**

# Acknowledgments

Everyone in our life serves a purpose, even if we don't see it at the time. This book is to all those who hurt me and ultimately helped shape the strong woman I've become.

To the kids who wouldn't play with me because I was weird and different. To the books who were my friends instead, especially the characters within the Babysitter's Club, Sweet Valley Twins, and Little House on the Prairie. To the boyfriends who dumped me, the ex-husband who shattered my self-esteem, the bio dad who didn't think I was worth sticking around for.

But also, to those who saw value in me, who lifted me up when others pushed me down. To my mom, who risked a lot in the early days to keep me safe. To the father who fell in love with first my mom, then me, adopting us both and making us a family. To my siblings, who are weird and obviously not as cool as I am but who, despite the rivalry, still love me as I love them.

To the friends who have come and gone, but especially to those who have stayed. To Mallory, Megan, Jasmine, Angi, Ines, and Becky, who are crucial as both friends and supporters of my writing.

To Mr. Storm, who taught me what it meant to love—and perhaps more importantly how to be loved, even when we don't feel we deserve it.

To my four-year-old daughter, who tells me, "You can do it, if you just try your best" apropos to nothing. Who makes me smile, laugh, and know beyond the shadow of a doubt that I am blessed.

To my six dogs, because I am just a touch crazy, but that's okay because I get lots and lots of puppy cuddles. And I guess to the cat, too.

To my readers. None of this is possible without you!

Everyone who has passed through my life has shaped the person—and the author—I've become, and this book is theirs. It's yours. It's ours together.

Thank you.